The Fountain of Death
(A Perfectly Silly Mystery)
by Kerry Marie Sloan

STARGAZER BOOKS
Philadelphia

STARGAZER
BOOKS

This STARGAZER BOOKS paperback edition August 2017

STARGAZER BOOKS and the STARGAZER BOOKS logo
are trademarks of STARGAZER BOOKS LLC.

For information about special discounts for bulk purchases,
book signings, and talks by the author please contact

Special Events - Stargazer Books
info@stargazerbooks.com
or visit our website
www.stargazerbooks.com

Edited by Linda Sloan
Design by Dan Yager

Manufactured in the United States of America

Library of Congress Control Number: 2017936662

ISBN-13: 978-1-944523-02-2
ISBN-10: 1-944523-02-2

To Elena, Dan, and my parents.

CONTENTS

PROLOGUE

     he village of Kingsley Green was abuzz with the news. An heir to the vast Kingsley estate had finally been found! For nearly ten years the ancestral home of the Kingsleys had stood, almost abandoned. Time and neglect had <u>transformed</u>* the hall into a dark and forbidding place.

Fantastic stories regarding Kingsley Hall abounded in the village. People spoke of an ancient curse, a vast underground maze, and a fountain that could foretell the future. Yet, no one really knew what dark secrets, if any, were concealed within the old building.

Before the discovery of an heir to the Kingsley title, many believed that the estate was destined to fall to ruin. But now, everything had changed. The new owner planned to take full possession of Kingsley Hall and restore the place to its former glory. For the inhabitants of Kingsley Green, this was a cause for celebration. But not everyone in the town greeted the news with joy. The evening of the announcement, on a hill overlooking Kingsley Hall, two men could be found, deep in conversation.

"Not quite what you'd planned, is it?" asked the first man, quietly. He was older than his companion and was gazing down at Kingsley Hall thoughtfully.

*underlined words can be found in "Katherine's List of Words You May Not Know" starting on page 105.

1

"Of course it's not what I'd planned," answered the younger man, in a soft voice.

"And why do you say what I planned?" he continued. His voice, although gentle, held a note of anxiety. "We're all in on this now, whether you like it or not."

"I suppose you're right," replied the first man slowly.

"Of course I'm right," said the younger man.

"What I don't understand," he began speaking again, taking up a train of thought that had been bothering him for some time, "is how this happened! I thought our plan was foolproof!"

"We've been over this many times," said the older man. "The Kingsley estate and fortune were being held in trust until a legitimate heir was found, or after the passing of ten years, and in that case..."

"I know," whined the younger man. "We don't have to review what we thought was going to happen. It's just that we came so close! I don't see how they could have found a real heir. We all thought the Kingsley line was dead!"

"I suppose we were wrong," sighed the older man. "I didn't think there were any Kingsleys left, and I never knew that there was a branch of the family in America. But from what I've heard in town, this new heir was an orphan. He didn't know anything about his family connections until Barnaby located him."

"Curse Barnaby, and the whole lot of solicitors! Everything was fine until he began meddling in this affair!"

"That's his job though," replied the older man. "We knew that things weren't going to be the same once old Stevens died. He was a good lawyer, but certainly not as thorough as this Barnaby fellow. From what I can tell, Barnaby made it his personal mission to get the Kingsley case sorted out. And I suppose he did, in a way."

"Yes," answered the younger man, "but not in a way that I like! And not in a way that allows us to continue as we had planned!"

2

"I still think we need to wait and see what happens when the new heir arrives," replied the older man, reasonably.

"Wait and see!" said his companion, trying hard to contain his agitation. "Is that all you can say? Where is that going to get us? And while we're waiting, what's going to happen to our plans?"

"All I mean," replied the older man calmly, "is that once the new owner arrives, there are bound to be changes. And maybe some of those changes will be for the good."

"No," said the younger man, a steely resolve behind his gentle tone. "There aren't going to be any changes, not if I can help it."

"But he is the new owner of the hall," protested the older man. "What he wants is going to get done. We might as well make the best of it."

The younger man glared at his companion through the gloom for a moment before moving away from him. Kingsley Hall loomed out of the darkness, eerily lit by the moonlight above.

"I'm not going to make the best of anything," mumbled the man to himself, as he glared into the night, his normally gentle features changed by emotion. "Kingsley Hall is rightfully mine, and it's going to stay that way, no matter what I have to do.

CHAPTER 1
ARRIVAL

A glorious summer day had just dawned over Kingsley Hall. Despite the early hour, a hum of excitement was disturbing the stillness of the peaceful morning. Seth Kingsley, the current lord of the manor, was expecting the arrival of his bride-to-be later that very day, and all sorts of preparations were in progress. Servants were scurrying about the house as if their very lives depended on it, and Seth was in a rare state of nervous excitement.

"Mildred, are you sure we have enough chocolate...and what about ice cream? Cordelia likes both and I don't want her to be disappointed," said Seth, worriedly. Seth, who had been hanging about the kitchen all morning, had already asked this same question several times, and the cook was at her wit's end.

"Sir," began Mildred, trying without much success to hide her impatience, "we have enough chocolate and ice cream to feed a small army."

"That's what worries me," replied Seth, his brow creased with concern. "Cordelia can consume as much, if not more, than a small army."

Mildred, a plump, middle-aged woman, had worked at Kingsley Hall since she was a child. She had been <u>devastated</u> by the state of disrepair that the hall had fallen into after Aloysius Kingsley's death almost ten years earlier. Seth had worked miracles since he inherited the hall, and the house was

5

grander than she had ever remembered it being. She gazed at Seth with real affection. Although she had only known him for a short time, she was already very attached to him.

"Don't worry, sir," she said, reassuringly. "I'll make sure everything goes smoothly for your bride-to-be. I've been at this hall for more celebrations and weddings than I can count, and you can be sure that yours will be the best."

"With your cooking there's no doubt of that," said Seth, grinning at Mildred. He took a deep breath and seemed to relax for a moment. However, relaxation did not last long as yet another worrying thought occurred to him. "Mildred," he said, "what about our plans for dinner this evening? Do you think that we have enough rolls and butter?"

Mildred sighed. It was going to be a long day. "Sir, we have more than enough of everything. You don't have to worry."

"And," she added, suddenly inspired by a wonderful thought, "I thought I saw that Mr. Pembroke, your neighbor from Blakesley House, walking about the grounds this morning. Didn't you say that you wanted to speak with him about something?"

"Yes," said Seth slowly, pulling his thoughts from rolls and butter back to the present. "Yes, I actually did," he said, with enthusiasm. "Thanks for reminding me. That will be the perfect thing. I'll go find Percy!"

Seth set off, all thoughts of Mildred, chocolate, and rolls gone from his head. Mildred shook her head at the retreating figure of Seth as she continued her work in the kitchen. He would be out of her hair for a little while at least. Despite her genuine liking for Seth, she had to admit that he was not too smart.

"All beauty and no brains," she sighed. "Just like all the Kingsleys."

*****

"Are you sure we're in the right place?" Katherine asked her cousin yet again, as their small car swerved onto the long circular drive that graced the front of Kingsley Hall.

"Of course we are," said Cordelia, with a light laugh. "I'd know this place anywhere from all of Seth's descriptions. It's quite nice, isn't it?" she said happily, as she slammed her foot down hard on the gas pedal.

"Oops...sorry...I thought that was the brake," Cordelia giggled as she tried to slow the car down. "I keep getting mixed up."

"That's okay," said Katherine, through clenched teeth. She was trying her best to ignore her cousin's <u>horrific</u> driving, but it was a losing battle. She should have never agreed to let Cordelia drive!

"I hate to mention it," added Katherine, trying to sound calm, "but should we be concerned about those two men in the front yard shooting rifles at us?"

"Oh, don't be such a ninny," replied Cordelia, with another giggle. "You worry too much!"

Before Katherine could come up with an answer, one of the men in the front of the house began running furiously towards them, gun still in hand. As soon as she caught sight of the man, Cordelia squealed with delight and quickly turned the car off the paved drive into a flowerbed, coming to a sudden stop only a few feet from the side of Kingsley Hall.

Katherine took a deep breath, trying to regain her composure after Cordelia's latest demonstration of her driving "skills." Before she could settle her nerves, a gunshot rang out.

"You're sure you aren't worried about the rifles?" asked Katherine again.

"Would you stop being so serious about everything?" answered Cordelia, as she hopped out of the car. "It's Seth! He's certainly not going to kill us."

"Not on purpose," said Katherine, under her breath.

"My dear, dear marshmallow puff!" shouted Seth Kingsley happily, as soon as Cordelia emerged from the car. A look of doglike devotion and perfect happiness overspread his features.

"My little chocolate torte!" responded Cordelia. "How I've missed you!" She ran into his outstretched arms, and the two clasped each other close, completely content in their long awaited reunion.

"Ah, Katherine," said Seth happily, as he caught sight of her standing by the side of the car. "I'm so glad you're here. It's been such a long time!"

"Almost a year since we last saw you in America," responded Katherine, with a smile. "It's so good to see you again," she said, as she took his hand.

"But we weren't expecting you so early!" Seth said, a shade of concern passing over his face, as he looked from Cordelia to Katherine. "I don't think everything's ready yet!"

"We wanted to surprise you!" said Cordelia. "We arrived in London late last night, just as planned. But instead of waiting for old Aunt Dorcas to join us this afternoon, we decided to leave early this morning. I couldn't wait. But we can help with whatever needs to be done. You don't need to worry."

"But lunch," said Seth, worriedly. "I don't think it will be ready for another few hours, and I'm sure you must be starving by now."

"Well, we did just eat breakfast..." began Katherine.

"Don't be so silly Katherine," interrupted Cordelia. "Of course we're starving. Breakfast was ages ago. But we'll be okay for a little while. I brought some snacks with us, just in case."

Seth breathed a sigh of relief and looked at Cordelia with love. "You think of everything dear, don't you?"

As Seth finished speaking, his companion, the other man who had been so wildly running about the yard when

Katherine and Cordelia arrived, jogged up beside them.

"Ah, Percy! So sorry old fellow, I'd almost forgotten about you! Katherine and Cordelia, this is Percy Pembroke, our closest neighbor here at Kingsley Hall. Percy, this is Cordelia, my fiancée, and Katherine, her cousin.

Percy, a large, <u>overbearing</u> man, flashed a charming smile. "Delighted," he boomed, as he <u>energetically</u> shook hands with Cordelia and Katherine. "Seth has told me many wonderful things about both of you."

"Percy was just showing me how to shoot a hunting rifle," explained Seth, grabbing the rifle which he had thrown to the ground at the sight of Cordelia. "Percy is quite an avid sportsman. He's going to help me restock the grounds with all sorts of wild game. We have plans for lots of shooting parties and hunting expeditions! Here, let me show you how it's done..."

As he spoke, Seth began swinging his gun all over the place, ready to shoot at whatever caught his fancy.

"Perhaps we should hold off until we have a few more lessons," said Percy quickly, as he took the cocked rifle from Seth's eager hands and began to unload it. "We don't want to frighten the ladies," he added, <u>condescendingly</u>.

"Oh yes, of course," said Seth. "You two city girls aren't used to all of this outdoor excitement."

"If you pull that lever it will be easier to unload," said Katherine, watching intently as Percy struggled with the gun. For an expert, he seemed just as <u>inept</u> as Seth. "Although I wouldn't presume to know anything about it, being a lady and a city girl," she added, with an innocent smile.

"Yes, of course," mumbled Percy, in annoyance, as he finally unloaded the rifle.

"Seth," interrupted Cordelia eagerly, "can we please have a tour of the house? I've been dying to see it for so long!"

"Of course, my dear," said Seth adoringly. "How could I have forgotten? I'm sure you two would like to freshen up as well. If you walk through the front door, Humphries, the butler, should be there. He's very efficient...always lurking about doing something in the butler line. He'll show you to your rooms, and then we can have the grand tour in a few moments. I just have a few things to finish up with Percy here first. We're off to speak with Farnham, our groundskeeper, about all of the details of our first hunting party..."

Cordelia gazed lovingly at Seth, "Don't be too long," she said with a smile, as she and Katherine walked towards the house.

CHAPTER 2
KINGSLEY HALL

few hours later, Seth, Cordelia, and Katherine were basking in the afterglow of a delightful meal. They were seated around a large table in the fancy dining room, finishing off the remains of their luncheon feast.

"I hope you're not too tired from the tour of the hall," said Seth, gazing devotedly at Cordelia as she scooped up some chocolate cake crumbs from her plate and deposited them daintily into her mouth. "It's a gigantic place!"

"It certainly is," said Cordelia. "But it's lovely too...I know I'm going to enjoy living here."

"And the meal we just had! It was remarkable!" she added, with a contented sigh. "If all Mildred's cakes and pies are going to be that good, I might start skipping lunch and dinner and going right to dessert. Why fill up on real food when there's dessert to eat?"

Seth smiled. Mildred had outdone herself with preparations for lunch. The meal was unquestionably a success.

"Mildred really is a splendid cook," said Seth.

"And such a nice, kind woman as well!" Cordelia replied, enthusiastically. "I'm sure I'll have lots to talk with her about!"

"I'm glad you like her," said Seth, happily. He was hoping Cordelia would approve of all of his arrangements at the hall.

"And what did you think of the other servants?"

As part of their tour, Seth had formally presented the staff of Kingsley Hall to Cordelia and Katherine, both the old servants who had been connected to the Kingsley family for years and the newcomers that Seth had hired upon his arrival.

"Well, I think Humphries is a jewel!" replied Cordelia, enthusiastically. "So knowledgeable about everything ... and such an attractive man! Don't you think so Katherine?"

Katherine smiled at Cordelia. Large meals always made her cousin extremely talkative. "He's certainly not handsome in the usual sense ... but there is something strangely appealing about him," she answered thoughtfully. "Although I can't quite put my finger on what it is."

Seth started at the two girls in amazement. "You're talking about Humphries the butler?!"

"Of course," said Cordelia, with an amused glance at Seth. "Unless you have several more attractive men named Humphries hidden about the place."

"Did you notice that Humphries is old, bald, and overweight?!" replied Seth. "He's probably the most efficient man I've ever met, but he is always lurking around and politely coughing...I don't find that very attractive."

Cordelia looked at Seth and sighed. "That's what butlers are supposed to do, you silly man! For my part, I think Humphries is fascinating!"

"Enough about Humphries!" said Seth in <u>exasperation</u>. "What did you think of the other servants? How about Farnham, the groundskeeper? I hope you didn't fall in love with him too!"

"Oh! That poor, dear Farnham!" Cordelia exclaimed. "Such a gentle, sweet face...just like a little baby! The poor boy seems to be so lost and helpless...I just wanted to scoop him up and care for him."

Seth groaned. "I don't understand! First Humphries and now Farnham! Farnham's an adult....he's definitely not a baby! Plus he's crazy...not quite right upstairs, you know. I don't know what you women see in him! You're just as bad as Mildred. She calls him her little lost lamb, or something just as revolting!"

Cordelia smiled at Seth's words. "You're exactly right. He's a poor little lost lamb. And that's just what I'm going to call him from now on."

"But what about the other servants?" asked Seth, anxious to change the subject from the fascinations of Farnham and Humphries. "Marguerite, Connors, and Jack are all came highly recommended, but I'd like your opinion of them as well, dearest."

Cordelia narrowed her eyes slightly at the mention of the other servants. "I'm not sure. I don't know if I liked the looks of that Connors. What did you say he was ... the chauffeur? He's much too skinny ... and he has shifty eyes. Have you noticed? You can't trust anyone with shifty eyes. And did you see that he was eating an apple when we met him in the stable? Why would anyone eat fruit when there's chocolate available? It made me suspicious."

"Maybe he likes apples," said Seth, reasonably.

Cordelia looked at him incredulously and then continued speaking. "And Marguerite! I didn't like the looks of her either. What did you say she does around here?"

"She's the scullery maid," answered Seth, despondently.

"Why do we need a scullery maid? I don't even know what a scullery is! Plus, she claimed that she was French, but I know she was lying. I asked her about les gateaux ... you know how I love my French desserts ... and she thought I was talking about some kind of toe infection, and not cakes!"

Katherine hid a smile. She knew her cousin too well not to realize that there was more to Cordelia's opinions than simple first impressions. Cordelia liked to drive her own car and was probably afraid that Connors, the chauffeur, would take over that role. She also knew that Cordelia didn't like attractive, young women hanging around Seth. And Marguerite, the scullery maid, was certainly attractive and young.

"Kingsley tradition dictates that we have a certain number of servants at the hall, but if they really bother you, I suppose we could ..." began Seth.

However, before he could finish speaking, he was interrupted by a loud shriek, which suddenly rang out from the kitchen.

"What could that be?" said Seth, jumping up from his place at the dining room table.

He walked quickly towards the kitchen, which adjoined the dining room, followed closely by Cordelia and Katherine. As they entered the room, they were met by chaos. It was clear that the butcher had just made a delivery, as there were various cuts of meat piled high on the table. The kitchen was full of people, all talking at once, and it was hard to tell what was going on.

Mildred, who was in the center of the group, was in tears. She was being comforted by Humphries and Connors. She kept repeating the same phrase over and over as she attempted to gain control of herself. "It's murder, that's what it is ... murder."

Marguerite was standing nearby, holding a large bag of laundry and looking extremely uncomfortable. The gentle Farnham, the little lost lamb, was next to Marguerite, an uncharacteristic dark cloud over his normally peaceful brow. He was staring at the table and scowling horribly.

Jack, the boot boy, was also in the kitchen, a place he often frequented. He was a scrawny young boy of about twelve, and he was thoroughly enjoying the chaos. That is, the chaos allowed him to snatch a few choice morsels from various cupboards and counter tops, chewing and swallowing each bit of food rapidly.

"What is going on in here?" said Seth, as loudly as he could in order to be heard over the din of the servants.

As soon as they noticed the presence of Seth, Cordelia, and Katherine, the commotion ceased as quickly as it had begun.

"Why, sir, we were just..." sputtered Mildred, still in tears.

"It's the meat...." interrupted Marguerite.

"Actually," said Farnham, with a fierce glare at Marguerite, "Mildred is upset because this isn't our order. It was supposed to go to Mr. Pembroke at Blakesley House, not to Kingsley Hall. It was left here by mistake."

"And, to make matters worse, the butcher tracked dirt into the kitchen when he was making his delivery," Farnham added, with a gesture towards a few spots on the otherwise immaculately clean floor. "Isn't that right, Mildred?" he asked softly.

"Why, yes, that's all it was," she said, with a sniffle.

"I'm sure we'll figure it all out and get everything squared away again, as soon as possible," said Humphries to Mildred, comfortingly.

"Yes, yes, of course," agreed Seth, happy the matter was being resolved so quickly. "Whatever needs to be done Humphries, you make sure it happens. And Mildred, please don't worry about these things. They do happen, even in the best run households."

A few moments later, Seth, Cordelia, and Katherine were back in the dining room. Order had been restored in the kitchen, and the servants had returned to their normal tasks.

"Quite a <u>conscientious</u> woman," Seth began after the three were seated comfortably again. "To think that she would be so upset by such a small matter!"

"Yes, but don't you think that was odd?" asked Katherine.

"Odd?" said Seth in surprise. "In what way? I didn't notice anything out of the ordinary."

"Well," said Katherine slowly. "I don't think that Mildred...or any of the other servants...were telling us the entire truth. Something strange was going on in there. Did you hear what Marguerite said about the meat? Mildred's the cook...why would she be so upset by meat? It doesn't make sense. Don't you agree Cordelia?"

Cordelia, who had been silent since the three returned from the kitchen, had a pained look on her face, and she seemed not to have heard what Katherine had asked.

"What was that, Katherine?" she said absentmindedly.

"Oh, never mind," said Katherine. "It's not really that important. I'm probably just imagining things."

"I'm sorry," said Cordelia. "I was just so distracted by that horrible boy in there. Did you see how much he was eating?"

Seth looked at Cordelia curiously. He hadn't thought that the presence of skinny Jack would upset her so much.

"That was just Jack, the boot boy. I was lucky to get him," said Seth. "I was told when I inherited the house that we needed a boot boy, and, according to the people in the village Jack's the best there is," said Seth.

"But I'm sure we don't need him! I don't even have any boots!" Cordelia protested.

"The Kingsleys have always had boot boys," replied Seth, "It would be a horrible breach of tradition if we didn't have one now."

"Well ..." Cordelia began. She lowered her voice to a whisper and looked around carefully before continuing. "I think we had better keep an eye on him. I can tell he's no good. No one eats that much without some sort of ulterior motive. He's up to something....I'm sure of it. And I'm going to find out exactly what it is!"

CHAPTER 3
KATHERINE, ANTS, and WILBERFORCE

he next morning, Katherine was up early, unable to sleep. Giving up on her comfortable bed, where she had been tossing and turning for some time, she had moved to a narrow window seat that looked out upon the gardens. Normally the sight that met her eyes would have filled her with rapture. The grounds of the estate were beautiful. But her emotions that day were in no way <u>harmonious</u> with the surrounding landscape. Katherine was instead sad and thoughtful.

The main focus of her solemn thoughts was Cordelia's upcoming marriage to Seth. "I should be overjoyed for her ... and stop worrying about myself so much," Katherine said to herself. Yet, despite her best efforts, it was difficult to feel entirely cheerful. Once Cordelia was married, she would be alone. And it was hard for Katherine to imagine life without Cordelia. Katherine and Cordelia were only cousins, but they had been inseparable from an early age. Like Cordelia, Katherine's parents had passed away when she was very young, and the two had spent most of their childhood together, at various boarding schools or at the home of their guardian, Aunt Dorcas.

As Katherine sat thinking about her future unhappiness, she almost laughed as she thought about how strange it was that she and Cordelia got along at all. The two were extremely different, as much in appearance as in intellect and temperament. Cordelia, with her blonde hair, sparkling blue eyes, and rosy cheeks, looked like a porcelain doll, although not a delicate one. She tended towards a pleasant plumpness, and her entire form <u>exuded</u> robust good health, vitality, and a laughing good humor. Katherine, on the other hand, was very slender, and had dark hair and dark, stormy blue eyes. She laughed and smiled much less frequently than her cousin, and lacked Cordelia's light-hearted openness. Instead her expression was normally thoughtful or guarded, and perhaps a bit melancholy at times.

"Sometimes I wish I could be more like Cordelia. Life would be much easier," thought Katherine. She sighed yet again as her thoughts returned to her present situation and the recent events that had so unexpectedly brought her and Cordelia to England. Katherine found it hard to believe that it was only a few years ago when things started to change. It seemed more like an eternity!

Two years ago, Katherine and Cordelia had moved from their Aunt Dorcas's house to New York City. Katherine, who wanted to be a serious writer, had hoped to find employment at a distinguished publishing house. However, after much fruitless searching, she had given up on finding a position that <u>befitted</u> her talents. No one wanted to hire an unknown female writer! Left with no choice, she had <u>condescended</u> to write an advice column called "Ask Amaryllis" for a well-known women's magazine. To Katherine's utter embarrassment, the column had quickly become so popular that it was now distributed to newspapers and magazines worldwide. Despite this apparent success, Katherine was frustrated and desperate to find a better position.

Cordelia, on the other hand, loved her job. Soon after their move to the city, she had found a position as a secretary at Kingsley's Confections, a large candy company. It was there that she had met Seth Kingsley, the company's wealthy young owner. The two, from the moment they had laid eyes on each other, had fallen completely in love.

Katherine didn't see how it could be otherwise. It seemed as if they had been made for each other. It also didn't hurt that Seth bore a striking resemblance to a Greek god ... wavy blond hair, piercing blue eyes, a perfect build ... he really was the most good-looking man that Katherine had ever seen! Unfortunately, his amazing good looks were not matched by an equally impressive intelligence, but Cordelia didn't mind. She wasn't much of an intellectual herself, having always reserved most of her brain power to the pursuit of locating and consuming chocolate. More importantly to Cordelia, Seth was kind-hearted, generous, and caring, and best of all, he seemed to enjoy eating as much as she did.

Katherine contemplated a brief courtship and an elaborate, chocolate-themed wedding, when suddenly Seth's position in the world dramatically changed. It was almost too fantastic to be true, but Seth was the sole heir to a vast fortune in England, the last living representative of the ancient Kingsley family, and the inheritor of a large estate called Kingsley Hall.

"And that brings us to where we are now," said Katherine, with yet another melancholy sigh. "Maybe Aunt Dorcas is right," she continued, "maybe I do think too much."

This was one of old Aunt Dorcas's constant criticisms, and was usually followed by the warning that women who think too much never find husbands. Surprisingly enough, Aunt Dorcas' predictions seemed to be coming true. As of yet, Katherine's experiences with boy friends had been remarkably unsuccessful. Katherine had very high standards for a husband. She was of a naturally serious and intellectual bent, and expected her husband to be her equal in intelligence. However, despite Aunt Dorcas' best efforts to introduce her to every young bachelor she could find, it seemed that no man existed who met Katherine's qualifications.

Suddenly Katherine stood up and gave herself a good shake. "Enough brooding for one day!" she said. "Things will work themselves out for me .... I just don't know how yet."

With that thought, Katherine left her room, ready to face the day and whatever it held in store for her.

*****

Katherine had almost reached the breakfast room when she heard Cordelia's distinctive high pitched laugh.

"No, no, no, Seth, you don't understand," Cordelia squealed with laughter. "Not aunts, but ANTS!"

Katherine groaned inwardly. Aunt Dorcas must have arrived! Aunt Dorcas, the two girls' unmarried aunt, had taken on the task of raising her nieces after the death of their parents. Katherine knew that deep down Aunt Dorcas was a kind, caring woman, but her outward manner did not display loving kindness. Rather, she resembled a gritty old tugboat, ready to take charge of whoever crossed her path and pull them in whatever direction she deemed appropriate.

"You see," continued Cordelia, "all of these women with Aunt Dorcas aren't our real aunts at all. They're what we call A-N-T-S...they're part of her group...oh I can never remember the name..."

"The American Non-Theological Tract Society," said Katherine, as she entered the breakfast room, where Seth and Cordelia were just sitting down to eat.

"Oh, good morning Katherine," said Seth, with a friendly smile.

"Would you like some cake?" said Cordelia, gesturing towards the bountifully laden table. "Mildred made a delicious coffee cake this morning...."

"No," Katherine interrupted strongly, with a hand on her stomach. "I think maybe just some tea."

"Ha!" said Cordelia, "I was right! I knew that third cream puff at dessert last night was a mistake. Didn't I warn you? You really shouldn't try to eat as much as I do..."

"Don't worry...I won't do it again," said Katherine, with a

20

weak smile. She took a sip of the tea that Cordelia had poured out for her, and then said, "So Aunt Dorcas and the ANTS have arrived."

"Oh yes," said Cordelia. "They're here."

"I suppose we should prepare Seth," said Katherine. "You've only had a few small doses of Aunt Dorcas I think. She's a bit harder to take in larger amounts....especially when she has the ANTS with her."

"She can't be that bad," said Seth reasonably.

Katherine and Cordelia exchanged a meaningful glance.

"Well, said Katherine, "that remains to be seen."

"Just so you understand, Seth," said Cordelia, "Aunt Dorcas' group, the American Non-Theological Tract Society...they hand out little booklets to people....about all sorts of useful topics...or at least topics that Aunt Dorcas thinks are useful. They cover just about everything, except for religion. Back when Aunt Dorcas founded the ANTS, there were already several other religious tract societies. Aunt Dorcas felt that it would be unfair to compete with them. She's very open-minded that way. And she's very devoted to her group. She thinks that she's helping people."

"She's not helping anyone. The whole thing is a bunch of nonsense!" said Katherine firmly. "But you can't tell Aunt Dorcas that. She's obsessed with her little booklets."

"But why did she have to bring her tracts and all these women with her to our wedding?" asked Seth, looking a bit confused.

"That's not all they're here for," replied Cordelia. "They're going to attend our wedding first, and then they're off to London for a huge meeting of tract societies from all over the world. Aunt Dorcas is very excited about it."

"Is that so?" said Seth, still lost. "But what are we going to do with them?" he added, somewhat desperately. "I don't see how we can keep them all entertained...."

"Oh, don't worry," interrupted Katherine. "Aunt Dorcas will have them organized about the house soon, making little improvements and suggestions. The real goal isn't to keep them entertained, it's to avoid them!"

*****

Later that afternoon, Katherine stuck her head secretively out of her bedroom door and peered carefully down the hall. It looked like the coast was clear. She breathed a sigh of relief. She had been waylaid by Aunt Dorcas after breakfast and treated to a long lecture on the necessity of finding a husband as soon as possible. It was clear that Aunt Dorcas had taken it into her head that since Cordelia was getting married, Katherine should be doing the same. One of Dorcas's loyal followers had even managed to leave a tract entitled, "The Perils of Unmarried Women in a Male World," in her bedroom when she was out. She knew Aunt Dorcas was expecting her to read it thoroughly so they could discuss its contents together.

"Yuck!" said Katherine, wrinkling her nose in disgust as she tossed the booklet into the small trash can in her room.

You are not going to ruin my afternoon, Aunt Dorcas," Katherine said to herself, as she cautiously stepped out of her room. If she could just get to the stairs unobserved, she might be able to make it outside safely. But, before she had made it very far, a screeching voice echoed down the hallway.

"Katherine!" the voice shouted. "Is that you? I was hoping to find you here. There are ever so many things we need to finish talking about!"

Katherine groaned. It was Aunt Dorcas, bearing down on her. There was no escape. Katherine looked around frantically, hoping to find a way out, when she heard a loud, urgent whisper coming from somewhere ahead of her.

"Katherine, quick, in here!"

Katherine looked around in confusion. She had certainly heard Cordelia's voice, but where was it coming from? Suddenly, she saw a small hand beckoning to her from behind an ancient tapestry that adorned one of the walls of the hallway. Unsure what to think, Katherine walked uncertainly towards it.

"Quick," said the voice. "Get behind the tapestry!"

Obeying orders, Katherine ducked behind the tapestry, and to her surprise, found herself in a small room with Cordelia and an unknown, elderly gentleman.

"Phew," said Cordelia, with relief, "just in time! Dorcas was about to nab you. She's been lurking about this hallway for hours. If it wasn't for old Cousin Wilberforce here I would have run right into her too. As it is, Wilberforce and I are much better off here."

"Here," said Cordelia kindly to the old man, "have another chocolate chew...these are particularly good. And, if I give you one of these, maybe you can give me another caramel cluster."

"Oh," said Cordelia, her mouth full of caramel. "Where are my manners? I almost forgot to introduce you! Katherine, this is Old Cousin Wilberforce, Old Cousin Wilberforce, my cousin Katherine."

Katherine looked at the ancient man standing before her with some curiosity. Wilberforce was a longstanding occupant of the house, a very distant relation of the Kingsleys. Despite Seth's best efforts the previous day, a formal introduction was not to be had. Any conversation with Wilberforce was dependent on his being found. And, since he tended to wander about the huge house at will, it was hard to pinpoint his exact location at any given time. But now, here he was! Looking exactly as Seth had described...odd, eccentric, untidy and just a little bit crazy.

Wilberforce gazed at her intently from under his shaggy, white eyebrows. His eyes were a keen shade of blue and he looked as if he wanted to say something particularly profound.

"I'm sure we've met before, under the old oak tree. But don't count the cows in the field before they come home to the barn. There are more fish in the sea than you might realize."

Cordelia smiled at him tenderly. "Isn't he just darling?" she said in a whisper to Katherine. "We met last night in the kitchen...we were both getting midnight snacks! We've become great friends since then. Don't mind everything he says. He doesn't make sense to most people, but I understand him. And I can tell he's extremely intelligent. He definitely has remarkable taste in food, especially candy. You wouldn't believe the dark chocolate nut clusters we shared earlier today. Really quite remarkable! And even more importantly, he completely agrees with me about the boot boy! You know, that horrible monster Jack! You won't believe this but Wilberforce says he's sure that Jack is eating the boots! Boots started disappearing right after Jack was hired. In fact, Wilberforce just told me that..."

Katherine smiled as Cordelia chattered on. Leave it to Cordelia to bond with Old Cousin Wilberforce! The man seemed insane, but Cordelia was obviously smitten with him.

Suddenly, Cordelia paused in mid-sentence. "Listen to me chattering on and on, when I'm sure you want to get on your way," she said.

"Well, at this point, I don't see how that's possible," replied Katherine, with a sigh. "Aunt Dorcas has the whole place covered. I was hoping to take a walk this afternoon, and have a few moments of peace and quiet. But it's not meant to be."

"Oh yes it is!" said Cordelia. "We can get you out of the house in no time, thanks to Wilberforce here." Cordelia glanced adoringly at the old man, who winked significantly in reply.

"He really is a genius," Cordelia whispered to Katherine. "It's amazing what he knows...including just about every way in and out of this giant old house. He even claims that there are tunnels and secret passageways somewhere under the hall! Just before you came in, he was telling me the most incredible story about the Kingsleys. Did you know that there's a curse on the family? Apparently one of the old Kingsleys did something unpleasant a long time ago. Anyway, since then, the Kingsleys have had spells of bad luck, due to the curse, and, right before anything bad is going to happen, the fountain out in the courtyard runs red...supposedly with blood!" Cordelia shivered as she finished her story. "Isn't that horribly delicious?"

Katherine looked doubtfully at Wilberforce. He was vacantly staring at the wall, and, every now and then, smiling and laughing to himself for no reason. "He really told you all that?" asked Katherine, with a meaningful glance at the old man.

"Well of course he did!" said Cordelia, rising quickly to Wilberforce's defense. "Not in those exact words, and not very coherently, but I can figure out what he means. We understand each other." She smiled tenderly at Wilberforce, before turning back to Katherine.

"Anyway," Cordelia began again, "if you go through that door and down the staircase which is behind it, you'll come out in the kitchen. And from there, you can walk right out to the gardens, without meeting Dorcas or any of her ANTS."

Katherine looked towards the far side of the room. Sure enough, just as Cordelia had said, there was a door in the middle of the back wall. The door was so small, and blended into the wall so well, that she hadn't noticed it previously.

"I don't think I would have noticed that door if you hadn't pointed it out to me," said Katherine in surprise.

"I know," said Cordelia. "It's a secret door. Wilberforce showed me this morning. I would never have found it either. However, now that I know about it, it's wonderful! We use it as a shortcut to the kitchen. It's very convenient for midnight snacks."

"I'm sure it is," said Katherine, with an amused glance at her two companions. "Well," she added, "despite enjoying your company, I think I'll make my way outside. I know I won't be able to avoid old Dorcas forever and I don't want to miss what might be my only opportunity today."

"Do you want some chocolates to take with you?" asked Cordelia with concern. "You might get hungry walking around out there!"

"I'll be fine," laughed Katherine, as she disappeared through the secret door.

CHAPTER 4
THE FIRST WARNING

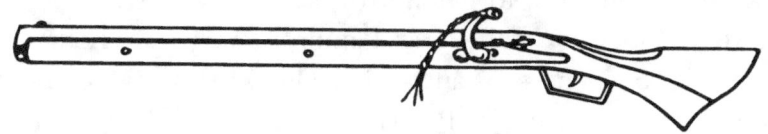

hat evening, a large party was gathered in the drawing room following the lavish dinner that had been prepared in honor of the arrival of Aunt Dorcas and the ANTS. Seth and Cordelia were seated near the fire, every so often breaking into uproarious laughter. Katherine, who was reading quietly at the other end of the room, glanced at them curiously. The couple, although quite delightful in many respects, had limited abilities when it came to humor. Katherine knew that their hilarity was best appreciated at a distance, which is why she had placed herself as far away as possible.

Katherine smiled to herself as she thought about the day that had just passed. She had managed to avoid Aunt Dorcas and the ANTS completely! However, it wasn't luck that had kept Aunt Dorcas at bay. Only a few hours after her arrival, Aunt Dorcas had come to the conclusion that all of Seth's servants were incompetent and were going to ruin Cordelia's wedding. So, instead of chasing after Katherine, Dorcas and the ANTS had spent the entire day harassing the servants. That very afternoon, there had been a violent culinary disagreement between Aunt Dorcas and Mildred regarding the menu for the wedding dinner. And Katherine knew there was more in store. Aunt Dorcas had a way of disturbing everyone with whom she came into contact. But for now, Katherine was off the hook. And she meant to enjoy her freedom, while it lasted!

"Aahh...peace and quiet," Katherine, said contentedly, as she settled herself more comfortably in her chair. She opened her book to begin reading again, when the unmistakable shuffling sound of an elderly aunt broke her concentration. She looked up and, to her horror, saw Aunt Dorcas, moving slowly towards her with Percy Pembroke in tow. Katherine groaned. She knew instantly what Dorcas was up to. Percy Pembroke, the <u>overbearing</u> oaf, had charmed Dorcas upon their first meeting that evening. During dinner, Dorcas had made several pointed remarks about Percy being quite a catch. And now it seemed that Aunt Dorcas intended to start her matchmaking immediately.

"Katherine my dear girl," boomed Aunt Dorcas with a significant glance at her niece, "I was just telling Percy here how interested you are in hunting. I thought the two of you could have a cozy chat, while I go look after these terrible servants. They're going to spoil something if I'm not supervising!"

Before bustling off, Aunt Dorcas pulled a chair towards Katherine and motioned to Percy that the seat was meant for him. Percy plopped down and grinned at her. "The man is all teeth," Katherine thought to herself, as he began talking. "How could anyone find him attractive?"

"I say, I didn't know you were a hunter until your aunt told me. Now, it's not often that you find a woman who's interested in hunting. I bet you'd like to hear one of my favorite hunting stories. It was only a few years ago, I was in Africa, and I was out very early in the morning..."

Katherine sighed, while attempting to keep a look of fascinated interest on her face. Hunting was certainly not a passion of hers, despite what Aunt Dorcas had said. On the contrary, she found it disgusting. A few years before, Katherine had written an "Ask Amaryllis" column in response to a question about hunting. She had done a fair amount of research to answer the question, and, upon completion, she had decided that she never wanted anything to do with hunting again. And now she was stuck with Percy, the world's most avid hunter, for what would probably be the entire evening.

As Katherine sat, listening to Percy drone on and on, she wondered how a man who could barely handle a gun had survived a hunting expedition to Africa. He didn't seem like an experienced huntsman, at least not what she had observed of him. It was very odd. Could he really be so accomplished? Or was he exaggerating to impress her?

Suddenly a line in Percy's seemingly endless story caught her attention. Whatever was he saying? She thought he had been talking about a hunting expedition to Africa, but, if so, his story didn't make any sense.

"The sun was setting and we were just about to quit for the day, when I caught sight of a gigantic tiger. It was a male, but larger than any I've seen before! Being the most experienced and talented hunter of the group, I went for my gun first and...".

"That's quite fascinating," interrupted Katherine, trying to sound impressed. "And all of this happened in Africa?"

"Yes of course, young lady! Africa, wild Africa! Really a very dangerous place, and not a destination for the weaker sex. But, speaking of tigers, that reminds me of another time when I was..."

Katherine was taken aback. If Percy had ever hunted in Africa, he would most certainly know that tigers were not native to that part of the world. How could he have seen, much less killed, a tiger while he was there? He must be lying!

Katherine looked at Percy thoughtfully as he began yet another story. She laughed to herself as she thought of Aunt Dorcas, who had been charmed with the man. For some reason, he was passing himself off as a hunting expert, when it was clear that he was just as ignorant of the sport as Dorcas herself. What was he up to?

Before Katherine could pursue this line of thought, a horrible, earsplitting scream broke the quiet evening calm of Kingsley Hall.

*****

Aunt Dorcas was standing in the middle of the library, which adjoined the drawing room, screaming loudly. She was already surrounded by a small throng of guests, ANTS, and servants when Katherine and Cordelia reached her side.

"What's wrong?" asked Cordelia, with concern, as she pushed her way through the circle that surrounded Aunt Dorcas.

"The jewels!" gasped Dorcas, shocked. "They're gone!"

"What jewels?" asked Katherine. "What are you talking about?"

"The jewels, you silly ninny!" Dorcas spat. "The Van Sant jewels...they were to be given to each of you on your wedding day!"

"Aunt Dorcas, please sit down," said Cordelia. "We can figure out what you're talking about later. Right now, you have to calm down."

"She's right," said Katherine, as she guided her elderly aunt to a nearby chair. "Just sit down, and breathe for a few minutes to calm down. Then you can explain what happened."

Marguerite, who had entered the room right before Cordelia and Katherine, looked at Dorcas with alarm. "I came in here to dust," she said waving her duster around vaguely, "and she was there, screaming."

Aunt Dorcas glared at the two girls and Marguerite. She realized they were right, but hated to admit it. However, she did pause for a few moments and tried to gather her thoughts before beginning to speak again.

"The Van Sant jewels, they're gone; well, at least half of them are."

"What jewels are you talking about?" said Katherine, in confusion.

"The jewels! They've been in our family for years. And they're to be divided between the two of you when you marry."

"But Aunt Dorcas," said Cordelia slowly, "you never

mentioned any family jewels. This is the first time either of us have heard of them."

"Of course I wasn't going to mention priceless jewels to two silly girls who looked as if they would never find men fool enough to marry them! Plus you two were always so irresponsible that I didn't like to think of you having them. But now, they're gone...or at least Cordelia's half! Disappeared! Stolen for all we know!"

A few polite coughs broke the silence following Dorcas's last pronouncement. "Ms. Dorcas, could you explain exactly what happened?"

Katherine and Cordelia turned around in surprise and saw the cool, collected face of Humphries, the butler. He was followed by Seth and Mildred.

"I thought they would know best what to do," said Seth, gesturing towards Humphries and Mildred.

"Oh Seth," said Cordelia, relief evident in her voice. "You're a genius! We haven't been getting anywhere with Aunt Dorcas, but maybe Humphries will have better luck. She keeps talking about jewels."

Humphries looked patiently at Dorcas, who was still in a state of shock at the loss of the jewels. "Now Ms. Dorcas," he began again, "if you could just start at the beginning and let us know what jewels you're referring to and how they came to be missing, then we could decide what the best course of action would be."

Dorcas took a deep breath and began speaking in a slightly shaky voice. "The Van Sant jewels are world famous. It's a small collection that's been in our family for years. I don't know what they're worth....to me, they're priceless. But I do know for certain they're a very valuable collection. They've been handed down for generations. They're to be given to the youngest Van Sant girl on her wedding day...and since Cordelia and Katherine are the same age, I decided to split the jewels between the two of them. I brought Cordelia's jewels with me from America and planned to give them to her this very night.

However, now they're gone, probably forever!"

"And when did you last have the jewels in your possession?" asked Humphries, gently.

"I had them in my room since this morning when I got here. And then, this afternoon, I hid them in the library so that I could present them to Cordelia during the party."

Humphries gave a delicate cough. "Did it occur to you that it might be safer to inform the household of the presence of these jewels? And perhaps deposit them in the Kingsley safe?"

"Pshaw!" said Dorcas, with disgust. "I've had the jewels in my own safekeeping since the girls were infants. I've kept them safe since then, and I didn't see any reason to entrust them to a bunch of no-good servants when I arrived here."

Humphries, tactfully ignoring Dorcas's last remark, gave another delicate little cough and began speaking again. "And Ms. Dorcas, did you think it was wise to leave the jewels in the library unattended while the house was full of guests?"

"You certainly are a disrespectful man!" said Dorcas, angrily. "Of course my decisions are wise! I didn't tell anyone about the jewels, not even the ANTS. And, as you can see, Katherine and Cordelia didn't even know they existed. I didn't tell anyone I was going to hide the jewels in the library, and no one saw me hide them. It's a mystery to me how they could be gone!"

Humphries gave a final discreet cough and glanced at Mildred meaningfully.

"Ms. Dorcas," Mildred said, as she took Dorcas' arm gently, their earlier culinary disagreement forgiven for the moment, "perhaps it would be better if you were to lie down for a little while. You've had a great shock, and a little rest might do you good."

"Yes," said Dorcas slowly, as she allowed herself to be guided out of the room by Mildred. "You're a lousy cook, but you do have a point. If I have a little time to think I may be able to figure out who took them."

Dorcas glared at Humphries for a moment as she exited

the room with Mildred. "That butler is just about the rudest man I have ever met!" She paused for a few moments, looking at Humphries more closely. "I really think I despise him....but there is something strangely appealing about him, isn't there?"

Mildred nodded her head in reverential agreement, her enmity towards Dorcas fading quickly. Any woman who could appreciate Humphries' charms couldn't be that terrible.

As soon as Mildred and Dorcas were out of earshot, Seth sighed and shook his head sorrowfully. "Well Humphries," he said, "I suppose we should call the police."

"The police!" Humphries replied. "Do you really think that's necessary?"

Seth looked surprised. "Of course I do. A robbery just took place! They'll have to question everyone, including the servants."

"Oh yes...of course," said Humphries, hesitantly. "I'll make sure everything is arranged."

"That's fine Humphries," replied Seth, as he sat down in the chair recently vacated by Dorcas. "I appreciate your help."

"Of course, sir....I do my best," he mumbled, as he hurried out of the room.

"I wonder what's gotten into him?" said Seth absentmindedly, as he gazed after the retreating figure of Humphries.

*****

A few hours later, Seth, Cordelia, and Katherine were sitting in the drawing room. The police had come and gone. They had interviewed all of the guests and servants, and then taken their leave, providing no further enlightenment as to the events of the evening.

"I wish the police had told us something," said Katherine. "I know it would help poor Aunt Dorcas. She's going to worry herself sick about these jewels."

Seth had a strained look on his face as he replied. "It's not just the jewels that are worrying me. I didn't mention this before because I didn't want to alarm anyone, but there have been a lot of strange disappearances at Kingsley Hall lately."

"What do you mean?" said Cordelia in alarm. "More than boots? What else has disappeared? Jack's not eating my chocolate too, is he?"

"No dear," said Seth, with a slight smile. "Nothing edible ... but quite a few of the Kingsley heirlooms. Several objects that are very valuable have gone missing over the past month or so. I've talked to the police a few times about it, but no one seems to be able to figure out what's going on."

Before either Katherine or Cordelia could respond, a loud crash and a strangled cry broke the stillness of the night. The drawing room looked out upon the main courtyard of Kingsley Hall, where a large fountain, as old as the Kingsley name itself, was located. The frightening sounds had clearly come from the courtyard.

"What now?" groaned Seth.

As he spoke, Cordelia and Katherine rushed outside, using one of the drawing room's French doors to reach the courtyard. It took a moment for their eyes to adjust to the dusky gloom.

"Oh no," whispered Katherine, as she grabbed Cordelia's arm for support. "Over there, on the fence," she gasped, as she gestured towards a section of wrought iron fencing that bordered the far side of the courtyard.

Cordelia gave a frightened squeak. There, before her eyes, was the mangled body of a man, gruesomely impaled on the fence.

"I think it's Connors," Cordelia managed to whisper, as Katherine pulled her back towards the drawing room.

"Seth," began Katherine brokenly. "It's too awful. Connors...he's on the fence. I think he must be dead. You have to go help him."

Seth gasped and ran out to the courtyard as quickly as he could. But, before a minute had passed, he was back in the

34

room, looking confused.

"There's no one out there," he said slowly. "And nothing on the fence. Are you sure you saw Connors?"

Katherine and Cordelia gazed at each other, speechless. What was going on?

"There has to be someone out there," said Cordelia, just as confused as Seth. "We just saw him!"

The three made their way out to the courtyard together. And, just as Seth had said, the place was deserted.

"But that's not possible," said Katherine. "He had to have been dead, the way he looked. He can't have just disappeared."

"Perhaps all of the excitement of the evening made you imagine..." began Seth.

"We know what we saw!" interrupted Cordelia, with a contemptuous glance at her betrothed. "And you better believe us or I will be very unhappy with you."

"Of course, of course," replied Seth, immediately cowed. "I'll get Humphries, and we'll have the police out again. I'll also try to find Connors. He must be here somewhere."

Cordelia smiled slightly and glanced over at Katherine, who had been very quiet for the last few moments. She was staring intently at the center of the courtyard, her face pale.

"Why Katherine," said Cordelia. "What's the matter?"

"The fountain," she replied, in a strangled whisper. "It's running red."

Cordelia and Seth turned their attention to the ancient Kingsley fountain. Just as Katherine had said, the water spilling out of the top of the fountain was bright, blood red.

"It's just like Cousin Wilberforce said," began Cordelia, excitedly. "The Kingsley curse....when the fountain runs red, a Kingsley will be found dead. That's what he told me just this morning."

"That's nonsense," said Seth angrily. "This must be someone's idea of a bad practical joke."

Cordelia stared resolutely at the fountain for a moment,

and then made her way directly towards it.

"Cordelia, what are you doing?" said Seth, in alarm.

Cordelia ignored him and continued on her way. She stood for a moment, looking at the red water pouring out of the fountain and then stuck her hand into the stream. She sniffed it, and then licked her finger.

"Hmmm," she said slowly. "Tastes like fruit punch. Not the best fruit punch I've ever had, but it's not bad."

Katherine and Seth gazed at Cordelia in amazement.

"What?" she said, as she looked up at the two. "It takes more than a fake dead body and some fake blood to scare me. Plus, all of this excitement has made me hungry. Anyone else need a snack?"

CHAPTER 5
THE POLICE AND A GUEST

I don't need to stay here while you search," said Katherine, cringing as yet another dresser drawer in her bedroom was emptied onto the floor.

As part of the police investigation of "The Great Jewel Heist" and the "Disappearing Body", Kingsley Hall was being searched from top to bottom. Chief Inspector Cornelius Blunderby and his assistant, Davis Jr., were in Katherine's room, overturning drawers, rifling through closets, and creating a general state of disorder.

"No, no, no," said Blunderby slowly, as he gazed at her craftily through his magnifying glass. "We want you to stay. We like to watch our suspects while we search their rooms."

"Am I a suspect?" said Katherine with a trace of amusement.

"Everyone is a suspect," said Blunderby sharply.

"Yes, of course," said Katherine. "I suppose anyone in the house could have stolen the jewels. Although really Inspector Blunderby, if I were a jewel thief, you don't think I would be silly enough to hide the stolen goods in my own room, do you?"

"Ah," said Blunderby, suspiciously. "It's interesting you should say that. Note that down Davis Jr. That's an important bit of information."

"Yes sir," yelped Davis Jr., as he pulled a pencil and a

crumbled, sorry looking notepad from one of his pockets. He lifted his pencil to begin writing, and paused for a moment.

"What was it you wanted me to make a note of?" he asked, looking uncertainly at Blunderby.

"Oh never mind," snapped Blunderby, in frustration. "You just aren't the man that your father was, Junior. Why, I remember cases where he had made volumes of notes before I even interviewed the first suspect. But you...you can't even remember your pencil or your notepad! I just wonder how you could be related to such a genius..."

Katherine watched the two men curiously as Blunderby continued scolding his unfortunate assistant. Inspector Blunderby, the older of the two, was portly and pompous. He seemed to regard himself as a crime solving genius, although Katherine had not as yet seen any evidence to support this view. Davis Jr. looked as if he was barely out of his teens....he was tall, gangly, and constantly tripping over his long legs. The two men, although clearly able to search a room thoroughly, did not seem to have the combined brainpower necessary to ask even one intelligent question. How were they going to be able to solve the crimes that had taken place at Kingsley Hall?

"Now then young lady," Blunderby said sternly, turning his attention from Davis Jr. back to Katherine. "I believe we're done here for the time being. However, I strongly recommend that you don't leave town without letting us know first."

Blunderby paused and glanced slyly at Katherine.

"Where would you have hidden the jewels, if you were the thief?" he asked, almost casually.

Katherine tried not to smile as she looked at Blunderby. Was he trying to trick her? His investigative skills were pathetic!

"Don't you think Davis Jr. should note my answer down?" Katherine said sweetly, with a significant glance at the befuddled young man. "Your notebook is over there, on my dresser," she added. "I think you set it there when you were emptying the drawers all over the floor."

38

"Of course he should note it down!" shouted Blunderby, glaring at Davis Jr., who was trying to write and pay attention at the same time, clearly a difficult task for him.

"Well...you were saying?" said Blunderby, looking expectantly at Katherine.

"I really don't know what I would do with the jewels," she answered. "Maybe I would wear them..."

*****

That evening marked the arrival of several additional wedding guests, none of whom, save one, knew of the unpleasant disturbances of the previous evening. Seth and Cordelia were attempting to keep the unfortunate events as quiet as possible. They didn't want their wedding to be tainted by rumors of the Kingsley curse.

The sole guest who was aware of the theft and possible murder arrived at Kingsley Hall quietly. Instead of immediately going up to the house and making his presence known, he lingered in the garden for a few moments, clearly enjoying the solitude of the peaceful summer evening. The man was middle aged and fairly tall, with light brown hair and a thoughtful, intelligent face. He was dressed well and had a quiet, reserved air about him, which made him seem aloof, although not necessarily unfriendly. The man, lost in his own thoughts, did not at first hear a cheerful voice shouting his name.

"Colin!" said the voice again. "I'm so glad you're here!"

"I've been on the lookout for you," said Seth happily, as he reached his friend and shook him warmly by the hand. "It's been much too long. But what are you doing out here all alone?"

"I needed a few moments of quiet," replied Colin, as a warm smile <u>transformed</u> his face. Although not as talkative as Seth, he was clearly happy to see his friend again. "It was a long day of traveling to get here."

"I understand," replied Seth. I'm just glad you were able to come at all. I wouldn't have called you unless it was very important."

"Of course not," said Colin. "But, as soon as I heard from you, I dropped everything I was doing and came at once."

"I appreciate it. I know how important your work is," said Seth, gratefully. "Would you like to go in? We can be a little more comfortable, and perhaps I can get you something to eat or drink? You must be starving."

"I'm fine right now," replied Colin. "And it might be better for us to talk out here first, where there's less chance of us being overheard."

"You're right," said Seth, <u>dejectedly</u>, suddenly remembering the events of the previous evening.

"Why don't you start at the beginning..." suggested Colin.

Seth sighed and ran his hand through his hair. Everything that was going on at Kingsley Hall was overtaxing his already limited intellectual capabilities. He still wasn't sure he had everything straight in his head, but he would do his best to explain to Colin.

"About a month ago, I started to notice a few things missing around the house. I didn't think too much about it at first. There are lots of Kingsley heirlooms, and I figured some of them were bound to get misplaced. As a precaution, I had the local police in. I didn't want any trouble once Cordelia was here. The police weren't much help, but, after their investigation, the thefts stopped. I thought everything was going to be okay, but then last night happened. First, the jewels and then Connors.....I don't know what to think now."

"The jewels were the property of Cordelia's aunt?" asked Colin.

"Yes," answered Seth slowly. "She was going to give them to Cordelia as a wedding present. And now they're gone."

"And Connors?" prompted Colin.

"Connors is... or perhaps I should say was... our chauffer. Cordelia and Katherine saw him last night in the courtyard, supposedly impaled on a fence. But since then, he's disappeared. No one's seen or heard anything from him."

Seth paused for a moment. "And then of course, there's the Kingsley curse! The fountain ran red last night...that means something horrible is supposed to happen. If anything happened to Cordelia I don't think I could..."

"Don't worry," interrupted Colin. "No one's going to hurt you or Cordelia. We'll get to the bottom of this before they have a chance."

*****

"Look out!" shouted Cordelia, as another poorly aimed dart flew dangerously close to Aunt Dorcas and a group of the ANTS.

"Sorry Auntie D!" she said, as she turned to Percy Pembroke, her opponent in the game. "Percy, I'm surprised! For a sporting gentleman you really aren't very good at darts. I was sure I was going to lose, but you're almost as bad as I am. I think your last dart grazed poor Aunt Dorcas' head!"

Percy turned red and coughed as he fumbled with his darts. "Must be out of practice," he grumbled. "And my arm's been acting up too. Old hunting injury, you know. I think it's affecting my game."

"Oh, of course" said Cordelia, with another laugh. "I'm sure that must be it."

Suddenly, Cordelia let out a great squeal of delight and ran towards the drawing room door. Seth and Colin had just entered the room.

"You're here!" she shouted, as she ran up to Colin and embraced him. "I didn't think you were going to be able to come to the wedding."

"I was able to get away at the last minute, said Colin, with a small, embarrassed smile at Cordelia's <u>exuberance</u>.

Cordelia grabbed the man by the hand, and dragged him over to Katherine, who was alone reading in a corner of the room.

"Katherine," began Cordelia impressively, "this is Colin Westbrook. He's one of Seth's oldest and dearest friends. He's ever so smart and does all sorts of top secret things that we aren't allowed to ask him about. We didn't think he'd be able to come to the wedding, but now he's here!"

"Colin," she began again. "This is my cousin Katherine. But she's really more like my sister."

I can't believe the two of you have never met!" continued Cordelia. "Katherine, I think you were off with Aunt Dorcas when Colin visited us in America, right before Seth and I got engaged. But I know you have lots in common. I'm sure you'll both get along wonderfully!"

With that, Cordelia turned her attention to Seth, describing in great detail and with dramatic reenactment her exciting game of darts with Percy.

"I'm glad to meet you," said Colin stiffly. Katherine attempted to smile at him, but was somewhat put off by the coldness of his manner. He certainly didn't seem happy to meet her. The man was positively icy!

"I'm glad to meet you too," she replied, unsure of what else to say.

After a few awkward moments of silence, Colin began again, trying to make an attempt at polite conversation, obviously not his forte.

"What is that you're reading?" he asked.

Katherine sighed in relief. Books were always a safe topic.... at least he wasn't talking about hunting, like the insufferable Percy Pembroke! "Dante's Inferno," she replied. "It helps calm my nerves. And it puts all of this," she added, gesturing towards Aunt Dorcas, the ANTS, and Percy, "in perspective."

"Hmm,' said Colin, a small spark of interest evident in his voice. "Dante is one of my favorites. May I?" he asked, reaching for her book.

"Of course," Katherine answered, handing it to him.

42

Colin flipped through the pages of the book for a few moments before handing it back to her. "It's much better in the original Italian," he said. "I always try to read in the original language."

Katherine flushed. She was at a loss for words. Foreign languages had always been her weak point. Of course she would have preferred to read the book in Italian, but she didn't speak or read Italian. At least she was reading something! And what right did he have to tell her what to read anyway? And in such a rude and arrogant manner?

Before she could reply, Cordelia interrupted the two with a loud groan. "Let's not talk about books right now. That's all Katherine ever does. I'd much rather all of you join me, Seth, and Percy for another game of darts. I'm going to win again...I know it!"

CHAPTER 6
THE SECOND WARNING

L ater that evening, Cordelia and Katherine were sitting together in Cordelia's bedroom, discussing the events of the day. It was their evening ritual, one that had started in childhood, and continued to the present day.

Cordelia had been describing Percy's lack of skill at darts quite amusingly when she suddenly changed the subject. "What did you think of Colin?" began Cordelia casually. "Seth and I really didn't think he'd be able to come. He's always off travelling around the world on mysterious assignments. I think he's some kind of secret agent, but Seth won't tell me. You know how bad I am at keeping secrets."

Katherine stiffened and looked away. Colin Westbrook was the last person she wanted to talk about. She knew Cordelia and Seth both thought very highly of Colin, but, after her short conversation with him earlier that evening, she thoroughly hated the man.

"He's alright," said Katherine coldly, "although his manners could use some improvement. He's certainly not a very good conversationalist."

Cordelia looked at her in surprise, clearly disappointed. "Why, Katherine," she said, "I'd thought you'd like him. He's the only one of Seth's friends who's smart!"

"Oh, I'm sure he's smart. He made that very clear. Although I don't think it's appropriate for him to go around telling people what to read. Dante's Inferno is just as good in

English as it is in Italian," she said angrily.

Cordelia looked at her for a moment and then burst out laughing. "I know why you don't like him! It's because you're afraid he's smarter than you! I bet you've never met anyone smarter than you before! Especially not a man!"

Katherine glared at her and then said haughtily. "It has nothing to do with intelligence. I just don't like him, that's all."

"Oh alright," said Cordelia, with another guffaw. "But please try to give him another chance. He's a bit stand-offish at first, but he's really wonderful once you get to know him. I'm sure you'll like him eventually."

"Let's not talk about Colin all evening," said Katherine, trying to change the subject. "Your wedding is in a few days. We should be talking about that."

At the mention of the wedding, Cordelia's normally sunny face clouded, and for a moment her eyes filled with tears.

"Why Cordelia!" said Katherine, surprised. "What's the matter? I don't think I've seen you cry since Aunt Dorcas threw out all of your candy when we were children."

"I know," said Cordelia. "I don't usually cry unless it's important," she sniffed. "But I think all of this nonsense with the jewels and Connors is getting to me. Plus, something happened earlier today that makes me a little worried."

"What was it?" said Katherine with concern.

Cordelia walked slowly over to her dresser to retrieve two small pieces of paper. "I found these this afternoon. They were both left in my room, sometime between breakfast and lunch, I think."

Katherine looked at the two pieces of paper, dumbfounded. "When the fountain runs red, a Kingsley is dead," she read aloud. She paused, and then read the second paper, "Marry Seth, meet death."

"Cordelia," she said gravely, "these are horrible!"

"You're probably right," said Cordelia regretfully. "I was trying to like them... you know how much I love poetry.... especially poems that rhyme. I suppose the subject matter is a little morbid. Usually I prefer happier poems."

"Did you show these to the police when they were here today?" asked Katherine.

"Yes," answered Cordelia, "but Inspector Blunderby didn't seem to think they were important."

Katherine let out a sigh of frustration. "There must be hundreds of intelligent policemen in England...how did we get stuck with Blunderby and Davis, Jr?! There's no way that we can leave the investigation in their hands. These two notes are clearly threats. I'm worried...I don't want anything to happen to you or Seth."

"There's more," said Cordelia. "I think my engagement ring was stolen today too. Cousin Wilberforce and I were making desserts this morning and I accidentally dropped my ring in some melted chocolate. I put it on my dresser so that I could clean it, but now it's gone. I only noticed this evening. I guess I'll have to tell the police... and Seth. I don't know how he'll take it. That ring is a priceless Kingsley heirloom that's been passed down for generations."

Cordelia looked as if she was going to cry again. Katherine walked over to the chair where Cordelia was sitting and put her arm around her cousin.

"Don't worry," she said. "We'll get this figured out. Everything's going to be okay."

Cordelia looked gratefully at Katherine, before jumping up at the faint sound of a creak coming from the wall behind them.

"Finally!" she said. "My evening snack! Can you believe that I ordered toast this evening! I never eat toast....much too healthy! All of this excitement must be getting to me. Soon I'll be eating apples, just like that horrible Connors!"

Katherine looked over to where Cordelia was standing. Many of the rooms in the ancient house had dumbwaiters, and Cordelia's room was no exception. Cordelia had been making good use of this convenience multiple times each day since her arrival at Kingsley Hall, mainly for snacks and extra desserts.

"What a wonderful invention!" said Cordelia, as she waited for her toast to make its slow ascent up to her room. "I wish we had these growing up!"

Katherine smiled, wondering what mischief Cordelia, as a child, would have gotten into with a dumbwaiter. She was about to answer her cousin when she caught sight of the contents of the arriving dumbwaiter. Katherine gasped in horror. Instead of toast, the charred, twisted body of a man was crammed into the contraption. The sight was appalling! Katherine couldn't tell whether the man was dead or alive, but it seemed as if he was leering horribly into the room.

Cordelia squeaked and sprang away from the wall, as she too gazed in horror at the dumbwaiter. After a moment, she gave herself a little shake and leaned in more closely, as if to examine the body.

"Cordelia, get away from there!" said Katherine, fear still evident in her voice. "It's Connors again!" said Cordelia. "He has that same shifty look that I told you about. And I don't think he's dead either. In fact..."

Cordelia reached towards the body on the dumbwaiter. Just as she was about to touch the man lying there, the entire contraption gave a large creak and went careening back towards the kitchen.

Katherine sighed in relief. She was glad that nothing worse had happened. She was about to reassure Cordelia, when her attention was caught by the open window in the bedroom. The window looked out onto the courtyard where all of the grizzly events of the previous evening had taken place. It was dark out, but there was enough light in the courtyard that Katherine could just make out the fountain.

"Look," said Katherine, faintly. "The fountain is running red again."

"Hmphh... I don't care!" said Cordelia, <u>disdainfully</u>. "Someone is trying to scare me....but it's not going to work! Let's get down to the kitchen. If we're fast enough we might be able to catch whoever it was. And hopefully I can still get my toast!"

*****

Very late that night, a strange scene was taking place in the stables of Kingsley Hall. Normally at such a time, the grounds of the mansion were dark and quiet. But tonight, there was a light burning in the stable and, for the past half hour, the space had echoed with an <u>eerie</u> chant.

"Our meeting is now concluded," sounded a deep, <u>resonant</u> voice from the center of the room.

"Praise to you and forever let us protect all life," responded the Kingsley servants. They were arranged in a small semi-circle around their chanting leader, Gregory Farnham. After a few moments of reverential silence, the servants began filing out of the stable, leaving Farnham and Humphries alone.

"Well," began Farnham, "I don't know about you, but I think that meeting went quite well. All of the other servants seem to be pleased with how things are proceeding."

Humphries looked glum. "I suppose you're right. But I still think we're going about this the wrong way."

"I don't see what you're so upset about," replied Farnham, a small cloud darkening his <u>serene</u> expression. "We talked about all of these things. What we're doing needs to be done."

"Of course," replied Humphries. "But I just don't like it. I think we've taken it too far. Seth seems to be a very reasonable man. Why can't we just talk to him? I think if we explained what we think..."

"You don't know what they have planned for this place!" protested Farnham. "Seth wants to restock the grounds for hunting... innocent animals are going to be slaughtered if we don't act quickly!" He paused for a moment and shuddered. "Just thinking about it makes me feel ill."

"Of course I agree with you," said Humphries. "But I still say we should talk to Seth. I don't want anyone to get hurt."

"It's out of the question!" replied Farnham, his normally mild voice cracking. "We proceed with our plan as originally

49

discussed. We have to make sure the dreaded event doesn't happen...or all of this will be for nothing."

Just at that moment, Connors, the chauffeur, skulked into the barn. He was still looking sooty and tirade and he had a scowl on his face.

Humphries and Farnham looked at him expectantly.

"Well," asked Farnham. "How did it go?"

"What do you think?" snapped Connors in frustration. "I told you it wouldn't work. Not after how she reacted to the first warning. She almost poked me before I made it back down to the kitchen. I don't think she was scared at all."

Humphries sighed and looked at Farnham. "Our plan doesn't seem to be working..." he began, before he was rudely interrupted by Connors.

"And another thing," began Connors. "What's all of this about jewel thefts? That wasn't part of the original plan. If we're making a profit with this little venture then I think the proceeds should be split accordingly."

"I don't know what you're talking about," said Farnham in astonishment. "The jewelry has nothing to do with us. Our cause is pure! You don't think I've been the one stealing from Kingsley Hall, do you?!"

"You're the one always saying that our group needs money. Doesn't it make sense that you might take it upon yourself to find some?" retorted Connors.

"Enough!" said Humphries. "The theft of the jewelry is not in any way related to our endeavor. I think we all know that. What we need to figure out now is how we're going to accomplish our goal since our plan to scare Cordelia doesn't seem to be working.

"Don't worry," said Farnham, with a dark smile on his normally angelic face. "I have a back-up plan. A friend of mine from London, very high up in the organization, is coming here tomorrow. I told Seth he's here to help with the wedding preparations. But he's actually going to help us ensure that the wedding never takes place!"

CHAPTER 7
THE DETECTIVES

"I'm glad you asked us here this morning," boomed Inspector Blunderby, as he bounded into the room with Davis, Jr in tow. "I have extremely important news."

Cordelia and Seth were sitting in a small parlor off the main drawing room. They both looked concerned, and the dramatic entrance of the bumbling Blunderby seemed only to increase their worries.

"The reason we wanted to speak with you," began Seth, "is because there have been a few more unpleasant disturbances. Last night..."

"It's of no importance," interrupted Blunderby, with a dismissive wave of his hand. "I've already solved the mystery."

"But my ring...it was stolen yesterday..." began Cordelia.

"It doesn't matter in the slightest," interrupted Blunderby, imperiously.

"And Connors," tried Cordelia again. "He showed up last night in the dumb waiter."

"It's of absolutely no consequence," said Blunderby brusquely.

Seth and Cordelia exchanged a bewildered glance. This is not what they had expected from the police.

"Well," asked Seth tentatively, "are you going to tell us your solution?"

"Of course, of course," said Blunderby, puffing himself up

to immense proportions. "Davis," he barked at his underling, "your notes please."

Davis started, looked around the room in a confused manner, and finally crammed his long arm into his pocket, from which he retrieved a sad looking piece of wrinkled notepaper.

"Here you go, sir," he squeaked.

Blunderby snatched the paper and started to read in a loud, solemn voice, "Inspector B is a ninny."

"Davis, Jr!" Blunderby shouted angrily. "What is the meaning of this?! Your father would be ashamed of you!"

"Sorry sir," squeaked Davis. "Wrong paper! Here you go," he said, offering up another wad of crumbled paper.

Blunderby glared at the unfortunate youth for a few moments, shook his head in disgust, and then began reading. "The culprit in the case of the 'Great Jewel Heist' and 'The Disappearing Body' is....." Blunderby paused dramatically, "Katherine Van Sant!"

Cordelia and Seth stared at Blunderby, speechless.

"What do you mean?" said Cordelia after a few moments. "I don't think I understand."

"I mean exactly what I said....your cousin, Katherine Van Sant, is behind all of the sinister events that have been taking place at Kingsley Hall."

"But that's impossible! What proof do you have?" asked Cordelia, in disbelief.

"Proof!" scoffed Blunderby. "Piffle! Just look at her! I knew she was guilty from the first time I talked to her."

"I don't believe it," said Cordelia firmly.

"That's understandable. The solution wouldn't be as apparent to a person without experience in the detecting business," said Blunderby condescendingly. "I'm known in the force for my brilliant flashes of intuition."

Seth was still staring at the man, dumbfounded. He looked as if he was trying very hard to grasp everything Blunderby had said, but with no success. "But what about the earlier robberies?" he asked finally. "Katherine wasn't even here. How could she be involved in those?"

"An accomplice!" said Blunderby, triumphantly. "She's been working with someone. Take this Colin Westbrook fellow...he would be a likely suspect. I don't like the looks of him either. Take my word for it, they're in on it together."

"Colin Westbrook?" said Seth dumbly. "That's impossible!"

"Anything is possible, my dear fellow," said Blunderby. "You learn that in my line of work. Now, would you like me to arrest them now, or should I wait until later this evening?"

"Not now!" Cordelia almost shouted. "Inspector Blunderby, please just give us a few more days. We're getting married on Saturday. We've been trying to keep the entire investigation as quiet as possible. Can't you make the arrests after the wedding?"

Blunderby looked doubtful. "That would be highly irregular. They may try to escape before then."

"Please," said Cordelia again. "We don't want our wedding to be tainted with any type of scandal."

Blunderby thought for a few moments before replying. "Alright. I'll let you have a few more days....but that's all. No mercy after the wedding."

With that, Blunderby and Davis, Jr. made their way out of the room. As soon as the two men were gone, Seth groaned and looked at Cordelia in despair. His head was whirling. He couldn't understand what was going on, but it seemed that the police, his last hope, had only made things worse.

"What are we going to do?" he asked Cordelia.

"Leave it to me..." she said, slowly. "I'm working on a plan. And it definitely doesn't involve the police."

Cordelia paused for a moment, deep in thought. "Blunderby might have given us the key to solving this whole mystery... Katherine and Colin working together!"

*****

"Katherine!" said Aunt Dorcas, "just the person we were looking for!"

Katherine sighed as she saw Aunt Dorcas steaming majestically towards her, with Percy Pembroke close behind.

Katherine was in the library, reading as usual. She had hoped to find some morning solitude after the previous evening's excitement, but it looked as if Aunt Dorcas had other plans for her.

"I was just telling Percy about one of the society's latest tracts," she said, beaming at him. "It's called "Girls Gone Wrong: The Social and Economic Dangers of Old Maids." Percy thinks it's going to be one of our most popular, don't you dear?"

Percy smiled at the old woman. "Of course," he said. "Young girls, and perhaps not quite so young girls," he added, with a significant wink at Dorcas, "should be married."

Dorcas giggled. "You silly man! I'm much too old to think of marriage, but a young girl like Katherine here should be thinking about it."

Katherine looked at the two, somewhat sickened. She had never seen Dorcas flirting with anyone before, and it was not a pretty sight. And Percy...why the man was just eating it up!

"All young women should be married," he said firmly. "It's their proper role in life. Leave the rough and tumble world to us men."

"Exactly what I think," said Dorcas approvingly, with a stern glance at Katherine. "Now Katherine," began Dorcas, "Percy was just saying he was going to take a nice, long walk in the garden this morning. I know how much you enjoy walking, so I thought the two of you could..."

Before Dorcas could finish Cordelia burst into the room. "Katherine!" she shouted. "There you are! I've been looking all over for you. I need your help."

"Actually," said Dorcas, with a scowl in Cordelia's direction, "Katherine was just leaving. She's taking a walk with

Percy and won't be back for at least several hours."

"Sorry Auntie D," said Cordelia, grabbing Katherine by the hand and pulling her out of the room. "It's an emergency!"

"Thank you so much,' said Katherine, with a sigh of relief, as soon as the two were in the hall. "That was close. I almost got stuck with Percy for the entire morning. I'm glad you came in when you did."

"You're welcome," said Cordelia. "But I wasn't lying. I really do need your help."

"Oh," replied Katherine, in surprise. "What for?"

"Wait until we get to the drawing room," replied Cordelia. "Seth is there, and he'll help me to explain."

As the two made their way into the drawing room, Katherine stiffened at the sight of Colin Westbrook. She hadn't expected to see him in the room, but there he was, deep in conversation with Seth.

"Ah," said Seth happily. "There you are. Have you asked her yet?"

"No, not yet," said Cordelia, with a worried glance at Katherine.

Cordelia took a deep breath and plunged right in. "The police think that you and Colin are the thieves behind the robberies and everything else that's been going on here. We know they're wrong, and we want you to solve the mystery for us...together."

"What?!" said Katherine, shocked. "The police think I'm...we're guilty? How is that even possible?"

"You've met Blunderby," said Cordelia. "He's not really the brightest man."

"That's true," said Katherine, attempting to take it all in.

"And you want us," she nodded towards Colin, "to solve the crime?"

"Please," said Cordelia, "you're the only ones who can help us. Colin's already agreed to the plan, we just need you."

Katherine thought for a moment. After the events of the last night, she had already decided to do some investigating of her own. The police certainly weren't going to solve the case! However, she hadn't planned on being forced to work with the <u>insufferable</u> Colin. But, after Cordelia's heartfelt request, and the need to clear her own name, there didn't seem to be a choice.

"Alright," Katherine said slowly. "I'll do it."

Katherine tried to smile at Colin, but he only returned her gaze with a chilly stare.

"Under the circumstances," said Colin. "Don't you think it might be best to postpone the wedding? At least until we clear everything up?"

"No," replied Seth, worriedly. "It's not possible. We can't postpone the wedding. I have to be married by Saturday or something happens with the inheritance. It's all very complicated. The lawyer tried to explain it, but I couldn't make heads or tails of what he was saying. You know I was never good at that kind of stuff."

Colin looked thoughtfully at Seth for a moment, his mind clearly working on some new problem. "That's very interesting," he replied. "We won't postpone anything then. And our goal will be to solve the mystery before the wedding."

"Thank you," said Seth, relief evident in his voice. "We know you won't let us down."

Cordelia smiled happily at Katherine and Colin. She knew if anyone could solve the mystery it was them.

"We'll leave you two alone now, to start working on a plan," she said. "Seth and I have to go calm Mildred down anyway. She and Aunt Dorcas had another fight this morning about the food for the wedding. Poor Mildred is threatening to quit if Dorcas doesn't leave her alone!"

With that, Cordelia and Seth left the room, and Katherine was alone with Colin. She looked towards him, unsure of how best to proceed. Fortunately, Colin saved her the trouble. He coughed nervously a few times before he began speaking, "We seem to have gotten off on the wrong foot last night. Maybe we can begin again today, since we're going to be working together."

Katherine looked at him in surprise. This was not what she had expected. It almost sounded as if he was apologizing. "Of course," said Katherine, softening slightly. Perhaps she could give him another chance.

"I think Seth and Cordelia are wise to disregard the police. I've worked with many brilliant policemen over the years, but these two don't seem like the best investigators to me," began Colin thoughtfully.

"They're not," agreed Katherine, ruefully. "I've seen them in action."

Colin didn't respond, and remained as he was, lost in thought.

Katherine cleared her throat to get his attention and then began speaking eagerly, "I was thinking that we could start our investigation by..."

"The way to solve this crime is to focus on the motive," Colin interrupted, clearly not listening to her. "We're dealing with someone who is not only a thief, but who is also trying to scare Seth and Cordelia."

"I really have thought about this a lot, and I have some ideas..." tried Katherine again.

Colin continued talking, as if he hadn't heard her, "The best thing for us to do is to start in town. I have a hunch that we might find out some valuable information if we speak with Seth's solicitor."

"But don't you think we should start by talking to the servants?" asked Katherine. "They're covering something up...I know it!"

Colin interrupted her again. "I do have some experience in this line of work," he said <u>dismissively</u>. "Now, if we're going to get anything done today, we should get going. Do you think you could take notes for me?"

"What?" said Katherine, taken aback. "What do you mean take notes?"

"Well," said Colin, "I'm going to need someone to write

things down while I'm conducting my interviews."

Katherine looked at him for a few moments, shocked. She could hardly believe what she was hearing. So much for his half-hearted apology! She should have known better! Katherine tried hard to swallow her anger. She was supposed to be cooperating with Colin, not fighting with him. But, she certainly wasn't going to be his lackey.

"It might surprise you to know that I have a brain too, that's just as good as yours, if not better," Katherine said.

Colin looked up in surprise, as if noticing her for the first time. "Of course," he said awkwardly, his face flushed. "I didn't mean..."

"I know what you meant," said Katherine hotly. "You're just like every other man I've ever met. You don't think women are capable of anything that involves intelligence!"

"That's not true," began Colin.

"It doesn't matter," replied Katherine, shortly. "I propose that we split up. I'll investigate in my own way, and you can investigate in yours. We'll meet back here later this evening, and we'll see who is more successful. And may the best man...or woman...win."

CHAPTER 8
DIVIDE AND CONQUER

"Just a little longer," said the small, dry man in a clipped, precise voice. He was staring intently at a large clock on the wall behind Colin. Colin had been waiting impatiently in the lawyer's office for some time. But, the man wouldn't speak to him. Instead, he continued staring at his clock, seemingly lost in the mysteries of time. Just as Colin began to despair of ever learning anything from this strange man, the clock began chiming the hour appointed for their interview.

"Ahhh," he sighed, contentedly. "Twelve o'clock...now we can begin. I do so like to keep to a schedule. Irregular schedules...very bad for the digestive processes...don't you think so? And this interview was so unexpected and last minute, I'm frankly shocked my digestion hasn't given out completely. But after Seth called me this morning, I couldn't very well say no, could I?"

The man paused for a moment and held out his hand. "By the way, I'm Tobias Barnaby, the Kingsley family solicitor, and you, of course, are Colin Westbrook, Seth's oldest and dearest friend."

"Yes," replied Colin uncertainly, as he shook Barnaby's outstretched hand. This man was certainly not what he had expected. "I think Seth must have explained to you that I'd like some information about Aloysius Kingsley's will."

"Of course, of course," said Barnaby, rubbing his hands together in obvious delight. "A fascinating case really, if I must say so myself!"

"I do so like to keep things organized," he added, as he began bustling about the room, fetching several notebooks and folders from the immaculately organized shelves that lined the walls of his office.

As Barnaby sat back down at his desk, he began speaking, in a friendly, conversational tone, "If you had seen this place after I took over from Stevens...he was the old Kingsley lawyer from way back! I don't normally tell people this, but he was not a very organized man," said Barnaby, with a shudder. "I had quite a time working through the mess of papers and files and folders that he had strewn about...no order...no system whatsoever. I have no idea how the poor man was able to get anything done with the deplorable state everything was in...."

"But about the will," interrupted Colin, trying to get Barnaby back on track.

"Ah yes," said Barnaby, arranging the folders he had taken down from the shelves on a neat pile on his desk. "That is what you're here for...now let me see..."

Barnaby picked out a large piece of paper from one of the folders and handed it to Colin. "That is the original will of Aloysius Kingsley. And, when I got here, that was the only will that anyone seemed to know anything about. Luckily old Aloysius had kept a copy at Kingsley Hall. It took me a month to find old Stevens' copy! I finally did find it...he was using it to patch up a cracked window pane in the front room. Can you believe that?! He just wadded up the entire will and stuck it in the window! Now, let me ask you, what kind of a man does that?! When I think of it I get the shakes..."

Barnaby chattered on, as Colin looked over the will. The document was very long and written in a dry, legal style that was almost incomprehensible. He could understand why Seth had been overwhelmed.

Barnaby was still talking when Colin looked up from his review of the will. "And the McAllister family? Do you know them? Quite well known in these parts...anyway, old Stevens was storing old Mr. McAllister's will in the bathroom...the Lord only knows why! It took me months to get that mess sorted out, let me tell you!"

"Ahem," Colin cleared his throat, trying to get Barnaby's attention. "About this will," he began.

"Ah, yes, the will," replied Barnaby happily. "As you may have gathered from your reading, the will leaves everything to the next of kin, besides a few minor bequests. On the surface it seems quite simple, but, at the time Aloysius made his will, and even after his death, it wasn't clear who his next of kin might be. Aloysius never married, and everyone assumed that the Kingsley line would end when he died. Old Stevens was supposed to have been looking for distant relatives, but any man capable of storing legal documents in the bathroom wouldn't be expected to make much headway now, would he? If I hadn't come along, Seth, the rightful heir, may never have been found at all."

"So besides the confusion regarding the next of kin, this is a fairly straightforward will," said Colin, "I don't see anything strange or mysterious about it."

"You're exactly right," said Barnaby, "a perfectly ordinary will, leaving everything to Seth Kingsley, Aloysius's next of kin."

Barnaby paused for a moment and then smiled at Colin appreciatively, "Not everyone can understand these types of documents, but you seem to have a good grasp of the essentials. Now Seth... he's quite a nice fellow, but a little slow when it comes to the finer points of the law..."

"Yes," agreed Colin, with a small smile. "But he did seem to have a vague understanding that there's more going on than just this will. He didn't understand all of the details, but he said something about having to marry..."

"Ah yes," interrupted Barnaby with a contented sigh. "That's where this whole case gets extremely interesting."

"When I took over this office," he continued, "there was only one will...at least one will that was known. However, as I began cleaning up the layers of disorder left by Stevens, I found two interesting documents."

"Do you know what a codicil is?" asked Barnaby, as he gingerly fingered two fragile pieces of paper that he had just removed from one of the folders on his desk.

"I believe it's an amendment to a will," replied Colin, looking at Barnaby curiously.

"Yes, that's a good way to think of it," he said, as he handed the two papers over to Colin.

Suddenly, Barnaby wrinkled up his nose, as if smelling an obnoxious odor. "You don't by any chance like fishing?" he asked.

"Fishing!?" Colin said in surprise. "Not particularly...but why do you ask? What does that have to do with any of this?"

"Fish should have nothing to do with the law!" said Barnaby strongly. "But Old Stevens was of a different opinion. I found the codicil in a rusty metal box filled with fishing tackle. Stevens was using it to line the bottom. You might detect a bit of a fishy smell. The other paper, the letter, was crumpled up in the bottom of a desk drawer. I think he was using it to organize his fishing hooks. You'll notice the holes."

Colin was already busy examining the two papers and barely heard Barnaby's tirade. Perhaps this is what he had been searching for...the clue that would unlock the entire case!

"It's a good thing I discovered these two documents," Barnaby continued. "Despite their unorthodox method of storage, they are drawn up correctly and have all of the weight of law on their side. As you can see, the letter was written by Aloysius not long before he died. In it, he confesses to fathering an illegitimate child some twenty years previously. The unfortunate mother was a maid in the Kingsley household, who died during the birth of the child. In order to avoid a scandal, the boy was passed off as the child of a local couple from the village. No one knew the truth, except for Aloysius, and I suppose it would have stayed that way, if he hadn't written this letter."

"But he did," said Colin slowly. "And apparently he

wanted to do something for his illegitimate son," he added, looking over the codicil.

"Yes," said Barnaby, with a smile of approval at Colin's quick grasp of the facts. "Before Aloysius died, he summoned the boy and told him the secret. And then, he had the codicil drawn up. As you can see, it specifies two conditions. First, that if a legitimate heir to the Kingsley estate is not found within ten years of Aloysius' death, the entire estate reverts to the illegitimate son. And second, if a Kingsley heir is discovered, he must marry within one year of inheritance, or the entire estate will go to the illegitimate son."

Colin thought for a moment, and then said, "It took so long to find Seth, that this fellow, whoever he is, must have assumed he was going to inherit everything."

"Exactly," Barnaby sighed, enjoying the legal complexities of the matter.

"But who is the illegitimate son?" asked Colin. "None of these papers mentions a name!"

"Ahh," said Barnaby, "that's the rub, isn't it? We don't know. Based on the documents that we have, it's clear he knows the facts of the case. And, as you said, he probably thought he was going to get everything. But since I found Seth, the situation has changed."

"His only chance now is if Seth doesn't marry," said Colin, slowly. "Exactly," said Barnaby. "The marriage hasn't happened yet...."

"And he's doing everything he can to make sure it doesn't happen," whispered Colin.

*****

Colin left Barnaby's office with his head spinning. It was clear to him now that someone was determined to prevent Seth from inheriting the Kingsley fortune. But who was this unknown heir? Was it one of the servants? Or was it someone else hanging about the Kingsley estate? And how was he going to find out in time? He was so close!

Colin felt a small pang of guilt as he walked down the main street of Kingsley Green. He knew he was on the right track, but perhaps he should have listened to some of Katherine's ideas. After all, he was supposed to be working with her. If only he was better at interacting with people. He was just so used to being alone!

Normally Colin wouldn't have cared who he offended, especially during such an important investigation. But, for some reason, he felt bad about his behavior towards Katherine. Perhaps he could make up for his rudeness to her. It certainly wouldn't hurt to ask a few questions about the Kingsley servants while he was in town. And he knew the perfect place to start...the local pub, the Kingsley Arms.

*****

"And then I'm going to make a chocolate raspberry torte," said Mildred cheerily. "I know that's one of Cordelia's favorites. Why the other day she ate almost a whole torte herself. I've never seen anyone who enjoys desserts more than she does..." Mildred chatted happily on, as Katherine sat comfortably nearby, sipping a cup of tea. It was late in the morning, and Katherine had ensconced herself in the kitchen about half an hour before, right after her unpleasant conversation with Colin.

Katherine only half listened as Mildred continued talking about desserts. She was thinking instead about all of the events that had taken place at Kingsley Hall over the past few days. From her first arrival at the house she knew there was something strange going on. As she often wrote in her "Ask Amaryllis" column, lies cover dirty secrets. And as far as Katherine could tell, just about everyone in Kingsley Hall, from the servants to the guests, was lying about something.

First there was Farnham...the man was so strange, and he seemed to hold some kind of power over all of the other servants, but no one would give her a straight answer about him. And then there was Humphries...he seemed like a rock of integrity, but once the police were mentioned he went to pieces. And then Marguerite...the French maid who wasn't French. And Percy.... the sporting gentleman who didn't know how to hunt or shoot a gun. Everyone was lying! How to make sense of it all? Katherine wasn't sure. But she knew if anyone could help her it was Mildred.

Katherine smiled as she looked over at Mildred, covered in flour and rolling out yet another batch of pastry. She was just like a sweet elderly grandmother, but a very well-informed grandmother. Mildred seemed to know everything that was going on at Kingsley Hall. Katherine thought that if she could just get her talking, she might let something slip.

But, so far, Katherine hadn't made much progress. Mildred was intent on her pies, tortes, and tarts, and seemed reluctant to talk about anything else. And, to make things more difficult, they weren't alone. Jack the boot boy was lurking about the kitchen, foraging for scraps. Every so often, he would stick his head around the edge of the table to gaze at Katherine craftily or to make hideous faces at her. It was a bit disturbing.

Trying her best to ignore Jack, Katherine was about to start questioning Mildred in earnest when Farnham and a strange, greasy looking little man that Katherine had never seen before entered the kitchen. Mildred looked at the two men and gasped in horror. They were both extremely dirty and their boots were caked with layers of mud. Before either of the men could speak, Mildred began scolding them.

"If you ever come into my kitchen again with such filthy boots..." Mildred paused and looked at the two men's dirty shoes, "you'll both be let go!"

"But," protested Farnham, "Humphries told us to come in here to get some twine for the..."

"I don't care who told you to come in here!" said Mildred furiously. "First you get cleaned up, and then you can come into my kitchen! Is that clear?"

"Yes, ma'am," replied the two men, embarrassed by Mildred's manner.

"Now get back to whatever it was you were doing before you ruined my clean floor...and don't come back unless you have clean shoes!"

Mildred looked over at Katherine apologetically as the two men left the kitchen. "Sorry about that," she said. "I don't get upset about many things, but my kitchen is one of them."

"That's okay," said Katherine with a smile. "I can understand."

"Who was that smaller man with Farnham?" asked Katherine. "I don't think I've ever seen him before."

Mildred wrinkled her nose and looked disapproving. "I think he's one of Gregory's London friends....Goldsmith or Goldhammer, or something like that. He came down to help with the wedding preparations. Gregory lived up in London a few years ago...made a lot of bad friends if you ask me. That city is no place for a sensitive young man like him."

"Oh," said Katherine, intrigued. "I didn't know Farnham had been in London. How long did he live there?"

"Only a few months," replied Mildred. "But that was long enough. We're just glad that he's back here with us where he belongs. He really is a very nice, gentle young man, but of course that makes sense, considering that he's...." Mildred caught herself, reddened, and looked away from Katherine quickly.

"He's what?" asked Katherine curiously.

"Well...he's just a sweet local boy, that's all," said Mildred cautiously.

"But let's not talk about Gregory all morning," she added briskly. "There are so many delicious things that I'm going to make for the wedding feast!"

Mildred walked over to the counter where several huge piles of vegetables were waiting for her, ready to be chopped and peeled. As she worked she threw the scraps into a small bucket next to her. Katherine watched in fascination.

Whenever the bucket was about half full, Jack reached in, scooped everything out, and crammed as much as he could into his mouth. Cordelia was right...the boy seemed capable of eating anything!

"So no news about Connors, I suppose," Katherine began again, hoping to get Mildred talking on another subject. "It seems as if he's disappeared completely."

"Well, he's been..." Mildred trailed off, paled for a moment and glanced at Katherine sharply. "I really don't know anything about it," she replied shortly. "It's too unpleasant for me to think about. You'd have to ask the police I suppose."

Another dead end! It was obvious to Katherine that Mildred knew much more about Farnham and Connors, but she wasn't talking.

"I saw Humphries when I was out walking this morning," said Katherine, trying a topic that she knew Mildred would immediately warm to. "I thought I was up early, but he was up earlier than me."

Mildred smiled. "That man is amazing. He gets up every morning well before dawn to take care of his mother. She's almost 100 years old, and he cares for her as if he were her servant. He's really a remarkable person...a saint if you ask me!"

"Mildred," began Katherine slowly, "have you noticed that Humphries seems a bit worried about the police being here? It seems to me as if they make him nervous."

"It's probably because he's ...," Mildred suddenly stopped talking. Her face took on an evasive expression and her expansiveness of a moment before vanished. "I don't know what you mean," she said flatly. "I haven't noticed anything."

"You certainly do ask a lot of strange questions," she added, with a sharp glance at Katherine. "I don't mean to be so curious," said Katherine quickly. "It's just that all of the disturbances over the past few days have been so unsettling. I assume the servants are feeling the strain too."

"That's true," said Mildred, looking relieved by Katherine's explanation. "I don't think any of us are feeling quite right, especially that Marguerite. She's been nothing but trouble lately."

"I think I saw Marguerite early this morning too," said Katherine. "She was bringing the laundry into the house with her. She's certainly a hard worker... always doing laundry or dusting something."

Mildred nodded slowly in agreement. "She is a hard worker... what with all of that dusting and laundry...I can't argue with you there. But she's not one of the old servants, you know. All of the others... Connors, Humphries, Farnham, me, and even Jack here, all of our families have worked for the Kingsleys in one way or the other over the years. But Marguerite, she's new... and she's been a nervous wreck ever since the jewel theft. I can't even talk to her she's so on edge."

"And she is a bit of a flirt," continued Mildred. "She was hanging about Humphries when she first got here, but I put a stop to that."

"Kissing in the parlor," piped Jack, around a mouth full of vegetable scraps.

Katherine looked at him in surprise. This was the first time she had heard him speak. "What was that?" she asked.

"Oh that's Jack for you," said Mildred, with a kindly look at the boy. She handed him some carrot peelings, patted his head, and then continued speaking to Katherine. "He keeps saying he saw Marguerite kissing someone in the parlor, but he can't remember who it was. He has a bit of an overactive imagination," she added, in an undertone.

Katherine looked at Jack curiously and then got up from her place at the table. She'd been in the kitchen for over an hour and hadn't been able to get Mildred to open up about anything. It was time to admit defeat. As she stood up, a small leaflet fluttered from the table to the floor. Katherine groaned inwardly. It was one of Dorcas' tracts...it had to be...advocating a healthy vegetarian diet. Mildred watched as Katherine picked it up.

"I'm so sorry Mildred," she began, "I know we said Aunt Dorcas would stop harassing you about the food for the wedding. I'll talk to her again."

Mildred had a strange look on her face. "Of course," she said in a strained voice. "Don't think anything of it."

Katherine stuffed the paper in her bag, making a mental note to speak with Dorcas. Why did she have to create such a fuss? Poor Mildred! Being persecuted by Dorcas was not a fate Katherine would wish on anyone.

Katherine sighed as she left the kitchen. She had hoped that Mildred would be much more forthcoming. All that she had discovered from her investigating was useless information... Farnham had spent time in London and picked up bad associates, Humphries was a saint, and Marguerite was a flirt. Nothing that would help her solve the mystery!

Katherine had almost made it to her room, where she was hoping for some quiet time to gather her thoughts, when she was waylaid by Cordelia in the hallway.

"Oh! I'm so glad I found you!" said Cordelia happily, as she grabbed her cousin's hand and dragged her into a small room off the main corridor. "We were just looking through Wilberforce's collection of old confectionary cookbooks. You should see some of the desserts in this book! Look at this one.... I can't believe how good it looks! And this, it's even better!"

Cordelia rambled on for a moment, before Katherine was able to interrupt her.

"Was there something you wanted?" she asked.

"Oh yes!" said Cordelia with a giggle. "Sorry, all of these pictures get me distracted."

Cordelia paused dramatically before she began speaking again. "Wilberforce has some information that he wants to share with you."

"Oh?" said Katherine, without much interest. As of yet, Katherine had been unable to understand what Cordelia saw in the man.   He was without question an idiot, but Cordelia seemed to think he was a genius.

"I told him you were investigating for us, and he got very excited.   He said he had something important to tell you," said Cordelia in an undertone.

"Wilberforce," she said, more loudly.   "Katherine's here, and she's ready to listen to your news."   Cordelia put her arm around Wilberforce as she spoke and looked at him adoringly.

"Aaah," he creaked.   "Yes, yes, yes, important news to share."   Wilberforce closed his eyes and paused long enough that Katherine was afraid he had fallen asleep.   And then suddenly, his eyes flew open and he looked straight at her.

"The servants....no meat!" he shouted.   And then, even louder, "The fake French one and the lying neighbor....kissing in the library!   They're no good!"

Katherine stared at the man, dumbfounded.   After a moment, he began speaking again, with the same intensity.

"Sticky fingers, sticky fingers!"

"Uh, Cordelia,' began Katherine.   "I think Wilberforce might need a napkin.   Were you eating chocolate?"

"No," said Cordelia impatiently.   "He's giving you a clue! Don't you see...it must be important!   He even made me write it down for you."

And Cordelia handed Katherine a small piece of paper. "They call him Sticky Fingers," read Katherine doubtfully. "But what does it mean?" she said.

"That's for you to figure out," said Cordelia sweetly. "You're the detective, after all.   We just gave you three clues.   I think that should be more than enough to solve the mystery."

"Thanks, I guess" said Katherine, disappointedly.   For a moment, she had hoped that Wilberforce would have something useful to offer.   But she was still right where she was when she had started her investigation that morning...nowhere! And what was she going to tell Colin when they met in the evening?   Perhaps he was right...maybe she should stick to taking notes.

70

CHAPTER 9
THE THIRD WARNING

atherine paused outside the library door as the clock struck six, the appointed hour for her evening <u>rendezvous</u> with Colin. She was dreading this meeting. Her investigations during the day had been fruitless. Now, she had to confess her failure to the very man who had wanted to use her as a secretary. It was going to be extremely humiliating.

Katherine took a deep breath and braced herself for what was coming. "Better to get it over with quickly," she mumbled to herself, as she entered the library.

Colin was already in the room, and he rose to greet her with what she thought was the shadow of a smile. Katherine was surprised. She hadn't seen Colin smile once since she had met him. She certainly hadn't been expecting a friendly welcome after their unpleasant disagreement that morning. But perhaps he was just gloating over his success... that would be more in line with his character.

"Katherine," said Colin, warmly, "we have a lot to talk about. But I think I owe you a real apology first."

Katherine was speechless. She hadn't expected Colin to be so friendly, and she certainly hadn't expected him to attempt another apology after his disastrous effort earlier.

"A real apology?" she asked, wonderingly.

"Yes," said Colin, reddening slightly. "I know I've been very rude to you. I don't normally work with other people...especially not when I'm investigating. But I should have listened to your ideas. You were right about the lying servants and guests. I made some inquiries in town this afternoon."

"Oh," said Katherine, not sure how to respond. Could this arrogant man really be apologizing to her? And had he really listened to her ideas?

"I'll tell you all about it in a minute," he said excitedly. "But first, let me tell you what I learned from Seth's solicitor, Barnaby. Barnaby showed me Aloysius Kingsley's will, as well as a codicil. As we already knew, the will leaves everything to the next of kin, which is Seth. But, the codicil leaves everything to an illegitimate son, if the next of kin isn't married within one year of being found."

"Oh my goodness!" said Katherine, shocked. "This changes everything! How did Seth and Cordelia not know about this?"

"Barnaby tried to explain it to Seth, but you know he can be a bit thickheaded when it comes to legal technicalities. Plus it's a very complicated situation. I think the only piece of information that Seth did understand was that his marriage needs to take place soon. But I still don't think he knows exactly why."

Katherine took a deep breath. Her head was spinning. "Who is the illegitimate son? Does Barnaby know anything about him?"

"That's the mystery," replied Colin, thoughtfully, "no one knows who he is. But it's clear that he's well aware of his rights in the case. Aloysius left a letter explaining all of his actions, including the fact that he communicated the contents of his will and the codicil to the illegitimate son right before his death. Barnaby thinks the son should be about thirty years old now. And he also thinks that he's most likely hanging around town, so he can keep an eye on his inheritance. That's about all we have to go on."

"But at least we know now who's behind all of the

disturbances at Kingsley Hall." said Katherine slowly. "It has to be the illegitimate son trying to stop the wedding. But who is he?"

"Before we go any further, let me tell you what else I found out today," said Colin. "I think it will help us. After I met with Barnaby, I thought about what you said this morning, and realized I was an idiot for not taking your ideas seriously. So I stopped in at the pub to chat with a few of the locals. I thought I could find out more about the guests and servants, and perhaps pick up some clues regarding the identity of the illegitimate son. So you see, I did take your advice."

Katherine looked at Colin uncertainly. She still wasn't sure she trusted him. But, maybe Cordelia was right... maybe he wasn't as bad as she had first assumed.

"Were you able to learn anything useful?" she asked.

"Oh yes," said Colin, with a smile. "The townspeople here like to talk, especially if provided with a few free rounds. And you were right... most of the Kingsley household is hiding something!"

"This may not have much bearing on our case," he continued, "but Humphries is leading a double life. He tells people that he takes care of his elderly mother, but his mother has been dead for about fifteen years. He has a bachelor's apartment in town, and several female "friends" spread out over the adjoining villages. He appears to be very energetic for an older gentleman."

"Ohhhh," said Katherine, understanding setting in. "I see now why he's so nervous about the police. He must be afraid he's going to be found out...and even more importantly, he's afraid Mildred is going to find out. She thinks he's a saint...I can't imagine what she'd do if she knew the truth."

"He's definitely not a saint," said Colin, "but probably not a suspect either. I don't think he would have the time or energy to mastermind a crime. Plus he's much too old to be Aloysius' son."

"Percy Pembroke was our next topic of discussion,"

continued Colin. "The townspeople had a lot to say about him! He's not the well off gentleman he claims to be. He owes just about every tradesperson in town, and he hasn't paid his rent in over two months."

"I knew it!" said Katherine. "And he's not the sporting man of leisure he pretends to be either. He has no athletic skills and he's lying about his hunting trips. He told me he shot a tiger in Africa, which isn't possible! But if he's not what he claims to be, then who is he?"

"I don't know," replied Colin. "The townspeople didn't have any theories about his true identity, but I think we can safely assume that Percy Pembroke is up to no good."

"And what about Connors and Farnham? Did you find anything out about them?" asked Katherine.

"Oh yes," replied Colin. "Connors is normally a regular at the pub. But no one in town has seen or heard from him since the disturbances at Kingsley Hall started...so he could be gone, but I have my suspicions he's still lurking about the place. I don't think we've seen the last of him."

"And," Colin added, "there's definitely no mystery about his ancestry either. One of his aunts was at the pub...she described his birth in great detail...a bit more than was really necessary, in my opinion."

"And Farnham?" asked Katherine, curiously. "What did the townspeople have to say about him?"

"Farnham's a different story," replied Colin thoughtfully. "His father and mother were locals, but both had connections with the hall, and Farnham has worked there on and off since he was a child. A few years back, he had some kind of a head injury and hasn't been right since. Of course, all of the women at the pub thought he was a little lost lamb that needed their protection. But the men don't see him that way. According to the owner of the pub, Farnham spent some time in London...mixing with some bad company. It seems he got in trouble with the law on at least a few occasions."

"That's exactly what Mildred told me earlier today," said

Katherine.

"In fact," she added, after a pause, "one of those London associates is here at Kingsley Hall now. I saw him with Farnham in the kitchen. Do you think it could have any bearing on the case?"

"Possibly," said Colin slowly, "there's something about Farnham that doesn't quite add up."

"But enough with my news," said Colin. "Everything else that I learned at the pub, although fascinating in the way of village gossip, was irrelevant to our investigations. And now, what did you find out?"

Katherine reddened. "Next to nothing...I hate to admit it, but I think you were right about my lack of investigatory skills."

Colin shook his head hurriedly and said, "Disregard what I said this morning. I'm sure you found out something that we can put to use. Sometimes the most trivial piece of information is the solution to the entire mystery."

"I don't know about that" said Katherine, doubtfully. "I spent several hours in the kitchen today talking with Mildred. I was hoping she would let something slip...but she didn't. I know she's holding back, but I couldn't get her to tell me anything. All I learned from her was that Farnham made some bad friends in London, which you already knew. She's in love with Humphries, although if she knew about his double life, I think she'd change her mind. I think she knows where Connors is hiding, but she wouldn't tell me. And last but not least, she thinks Marguerite is no good. Jack the boot boy claims that he saw Marguerite kissing someone in the parlor, but he didn't know who."

Katherine paused for a moment and then began speaking again. "Oh, and I also spoke with old cousin Wilberforce," she said. "I'm sure you've seen him about the place. A crazy looking old man?"

"Yes," said Colin with a smile. "He's waylaid me in the hall a few times already. He wanted me to try to some chocolates he'd made. At least I think that's what he wanted. He didn't really make much sense."

"That's the man!" said Katherine. "Cordelia thought he had something important to tell me, but it turned out to be nonsense. He said something about the servants and meat that made no sense. And he mentioned a French woman kissing someone in the library... I think he said the lying neighbor," Katherine paused for a moment, trying to remember his exact words.

"I suppose he could have meant Marguerite and Percy Pembroke," said Katherine, doubtfully. "It would go along with what Jack said. But I'm not sure if it has any relation to our case."

"And the last thing he said I don't quite remember," said Katherine, "but he wrote it down for me so I wouldn't forgot. Something about fingers... hold on a moment..."

Katherine reached into her bag to retrieve the note Wilberforce had given her. As she did so, Aunt Dorcas' tract, which she had taken from the kitchen earlier that day, fell to the floor.

"They call him Sticky Fingers," read Katherine.

"Sticky Fingers," said Colin slowly. "Now that actually does ring a bell... let me think... where have I heard that name before?"

As he spoke, he bent down to retrieve the paper that Katherine had dropped. Colin glanced at the tract as he picked it up and then suddenly stiffened. "Where did you get this?" he asked, harshly, holding the tract up in front of her.

"Oh that," said Katherine, <u>dismissively</u>, surprised at his vehemence. "You don't need to worry about it...it's just another one of old Aunt Dorcas' tracts. That's a vegetarian one, I think. I found it this morning in the kitchen. Aunt Dorcas has been harassing poor Mildred about her cooking since she arrived and everyone is afraid that she'll quit if Dorcas doesn't leave her alone."

"No," said Colin slowly. "Take a closer look. This isn't one of your aunt's publications."

He handed her the paper and Katherine looked at it more carefully. "Oh!" she said in surprise. "I guess it's not. This looks like it's from another group entirely, not Aunt Dorcas' ANTS. The International Society for the Liberation of All Sentient and Insentient Beings," she read. "It sounds even crazier than Aunt Dorcas' group."

"It is," said Colin grimly. "Crazy and dangerous."

"You've heard of this group?" asked Katherine, in surprise. "Isn't it just a bunch of vegetarians? How could they be dangerous?"

"The Society isn't a real vegetarian group at all," replied Colin. "It's a front for a very dangerous group of <u>anarchists</u> called Goldhammer. We've linked them to assassination attempts and bombings all over the country, all directed against the government or the upper classes. The group is led by a man named Oliver Goldhammer. We've been tracking him for years but have never come close to catching him..."

"Goldhammer..." Katherine said slowly. "That was the name of the man who was with Farnham this afternoon. I'm almost sure of it."

Colin looked at her, alarm evident in his face. "If that's the case, then we're in for more trouble than I thought."

Katherine looked at him nervously. Colin seemed so calm ... if he was alarmed then it must be serious.

"What are we going to do?" asked Katherine.

Before Colin could answer, there was a commotion at the door and Mildred burst into the library, looking as if she had just seen a ghost.

"I'm sorry to interrupt, but I didn't know what else to do," she began in a frightened voice.

"What's the matter Mildred?" said Katherine in concern.

"I was supposed to bring up a cake to Cordelia and Seth this evening before dinner, as a sort of snack. You know how Cordelia likes to eat dessert before and after dinner. When I went into parlor, there was no one there. Except this note."

Mildred handed Katherine a small piece of paper.

Katherine glanced at it quickly and turned white. She handed it wordlessly to Colin, who also looked it over. His mouth was set in a grim line, as he read aloud:

> *The wedding brings death*
> *To Cordelia and Seth*
> *Woe to all at Kingsley Hall*
>
> *PS We have Seth and Cordelia.*
> *We're going to blow up the*
> *house.*

"Have you told anyone else about this?" he asked Mildred sharply.

"No," she replied. "I came here as soon as I found it."

"Gather all of the servants in the drawing room. We'll meet you there in half an hour. We're going to need your help," he said gravely.

"Of course," said Mildred. "And you may want to know," she added in a shaky voice, "the fountain is running red again."

CHAPTER 10
SETTING THE TRAP

You'll never get away with this Farnham!" said Seth angrily, as he struggled in the chair where he was bound. Cordelia, seated next to him, was also tightly tied up.

"I say, Seth..." began Farnham apologetically, "I really didn't mean for things to..."

"Would you be quiet!" shouted Oliver Goldhammer.

He paused for a moment, looked at Seth and Cordelia, and laughed vindictively. "Hah! It's funny you're still calling him Farnham!" he said, mockingly. "Pretty soon it'll be Kingsley, once you and your fiancée are disposed of. I suppose Farnham was planning on inheriting the house too, but plans have changed and the house will have to go."

"Who are you? And what are you talking about?" asked Seth. He looked confused, as if he still didn't understand what was going on.

Cordelia, unfazed by the situation, immediately piped up, "You're not really going to blow up the house, are you? All of the wedding food is up there, and I was so hoping to try those little chocolate cakes that Mildred made this morning. And if you blow up the house I won't be able to eat any of them!"

"Stop talking!" shouted Goldhammer in annoyance. "I'm trying to concentrate."

He was standing a few feet away, fiddling with a complicated looking mechanical contraption that stood on a small wooden table.

"I bet that's the bomb," whispered Cordelia to Seth. "It's not really what I thought a bomb would look like. I always thought bombs were a little rounder and a bit more..."

"Didn't I just tell you to be quiet!" Goldhammer shouted. "I should have gagged both of you, just so I didn't have to hear your endless talking!"

"Oh I don't think the whole gagging thing would really work," responded Cordelia. "I could probably still hum, and I'm really quite a good hummer. You can ask Seth.... I've hummed for hours and hours at a time, some of the most beautiful songs...."

"She's right," agreed Seth. "She is a very talented hummer."

"For the last time, keep quiet or I'll make you be quiet!" Goldhammer snapped in frustration.

"Could you at least tell us where we are?" asked Cordelia after a few moments. "And then I promise I'll be quiet," she added.

"You mean you don't know!" said Goldhammer, incredulously. "The future mistress of Kingsley Hall doesn't recognize her own domain! We're in the tunnels that run underneath your stately home. There are lots of them down here....really almost a maze. Right now, we're sitting directly underneath your famous fountain."

"So Wilberforce was right! There are tunnels underneath the house," said Seth, in surprise.

"See," said Cordelia triumphantly, "I told you he wasn't crazy."

"Okay, now that you know where you are...be quiet, both of you!" said Goldhammer sharply. After a few moments he was again absorbed in his work on the bomb. While he was working, Cordelia gestured to Farnham to come closer to her so she could speak to him without Goldhammer overhearing.

"Farnham," whispered Cordelia, "I'm starting to think that this friend of yours is not a very nice man. And, if you really are a Kingsley, you've been lying to us," she added, looking reproachfully at him.

"I'm so sorry," said Farnham, two tears glistening in his clear blue eyes. "I've been lying to you since the day you arrived...and Seth long before that."

"But why?" said Cordelia. "Seth always wanted a brother! We would have welcomed you into the Kingsley family. If you had just told us everything from the beginning I'm sure we could have figured something out. We're very reasonable people."

"I thought what I was doing was right...it's all for the animals really, not for me. I don't want the house or the money. I just wanted..."

"Farnham, stop talking to those two morons and come help me with this!" said Goldhammer angrily, as he struggled to move the bomb from the table to the floor in front of Seth and Cordelia's feet.

Farnham glanced sorrowfully at Seth and Cordelia, and headed quickly over to Goldhammer.

*****

As soon as Mildred left the room, Colin set his watch on the table and looked at Katherine. "We have half an hour to come up with a plan. I believe we can do it, but we need to work together."

Katherine nodded her head in reply. She was still a little taken aback by Colin's newfound friendliness, but he was right. They had to solve the mystery, and soon. It was no longer only to clear their own names; Seth and Cordelia's lives depended upon it.

"Unfortunately, I don't see how we're any closer to solving the mystery than we were before we started our investigating," said Katherine.

"Ah, but there you're wrong," replied Colin. "We have all of the necessary information. We just have to arrange it in the correct pattern."

"Yes," said Katherine slowly, "but I don't think there is a pattern. Nothing makes sense, especially when you look at the crimes that have been committed. The warning notes, the fountain, and Connors's theatrics all fit with someone trying to prevent Seth and Cordelia's marriage in order to inherit the Kingsley estate. But the robberies don't work with that theory. Why would someone who thinks he's going to inherit the Kingsley fortune rob from himself?"

Katherine paused, deep in thought. "It's really as if there were two separate minds at work," she sighed. "And they're working at cross purposes with each other."

Colin was silent for a moment and then looked up at Katherine, excitedly. "That's it!" he exclaimed, as he stood up and began pacing about the room. "You've got it!"

"I don't see what you mean," said Katherine, in confusion. "I didn't solve anything. I just said that these crimes don't make sense when you look at them together."

"But don't you see?!" said Colin, trying hard to control his excitement. "That's just it! They don't make sense together because they aren't together. We've been blind this whole time! They're two completely different sets of crimes...one, the robberies, and two, the attempts to scare Seth and Cordelia."

"You're right!" replied Katherine, as realization dawned on her. "So that means we have a jewel thief and a <u>disgruntled</u> heir."

"What did you say was in that note that old Wilberforce gave you earlier?" Colin asked suddenly.

"I'm not sure what that has to do with it," said Katherine doubtfully. "But if you really want to know, his note said: 'They call him Sticky Fingers.' It doesn't make any sense to me. I really think Wilberforce is crazy."

"Oh but you're wrong!" said Colin with a smile. "I knew that name sounded familiar to me when you first read Wilberforce's note. Sticky Fingers is the alias of a notorious jewel thief. He's been operating throughout the country over the past few years...stealing huge amounts from the richest families. He normally ingratiates himself with a wealthy family, passing himself off as a rich bachelor, and then, with his accomplice, an attractive young woman, he steals everything he can get his hands on. Sound like someone we know?"

Katherine's eyes widened as she realized what Colin was saying. "Percy Pembroke and....Marguerite...are our jewel thieves!" she said in amazement, finding it hard to believe her own words.

Katherine's head was in a whirl, but she couldn't help thinking of Aunt Dorcas. She tried unsuccessfully to suppress a smile.

"And to think!" she said, "Aunt Dorcas wanted me to marry Percy. Won't she be sore when she finds out! She thinks he's God's gift to the female world!"

Colin frowned slightly. He wasn't sure why, but the thought of Katherine marrying Percy Pembroke, thief or no, disturbed him.

"Well you can be happy that you escaped from that unfortunate alliance," he said shortly. "But let's get back to our task at hand. We have our jewel thief...so who does that leave for our heir?"

"Hmmm," said Katherine. "If it's not Percy Pembroke, what about Farnham or Goldhammer?" asked Katherine.

"Perhaps," said Colin, musingly. "I know they're mixed up in something underhanded, I'm just not sure what it is yet."

"I think our time is up," said Katherine, glancing at Colin's watch. "The servants know at least some of what's going on. They might be able to fill in some of the blanks for us. But what are we going to tell them? I'm still having trouble believing everything!"

"Don't worry," said Colin with a smile. "I have a plan. We're going to set a trap my dear...and it will be fascinating to see what we catch!"

*****

Katherine and Colin walked into the library at the appointed time, but only Humphries was in the room. He looked worn out and tired, his efficient demeanor gone. He was pacing the room nervously and looked up anxiously when the two entered.

"The others should be here soon," he said, attempting to sound normal.

Colin walked up to Humphries and placed his hand reassuringly on the man's arm. "Don't worry Humphries," he said. "We know you aren't behind any of the events that have been going on here. And," he added, with a meaningful look, "your secret is safe with us."

Humphries looked up at Colin sharply, as if ready to deny whatever Colin was accusing him of. "We know about your other activities," said Colin. "But there's no need to worry. They have nothing to do with this case. What you do in your personal time is none of our business."

"Then," began Humphries hesitantly, "you won't tell Mildred or anyone else... and the police... do they know?"

"The police don't know anything," said Colin derisively, "and with Blunderby on the case they certainly won't ever find anything out."

Humphries looked at Colin gratefully. "Thank you," he said.

"It's the least we can do," said Colin, "but I'm going to need your help. We have a lot of work ahead of us."

"That won't be a problem," said Humphries, straightening up and looking at Colin confidently, his efficient manner returning.

The other servants were entering the room, Mildred first, followed by Jack. A few moments later, Connors, still looking disheveled, entered the room sheepishly.

"Connors! You're alive!" said Katherine in surprise. "We weren't sure what happened to you!"

"Been sleeping in the barn," said Connors shortly, clearly

unhappy with the entire situation. "Sorry about everything else," he muttered.

Mildred walked up to Katherine and Colin, tears trembling in her eyes. "I think there's something we need to tell you," she began. As she spoke she glanced at Humphries, still uncertain she was doing the right thing.

"It's okay," he said. "They need to know."

"I'm so ashamed to tell you this," she began, "but we've known about the attempts to scare Seth and Cordelia from the beginning. In fact, we've been behind them. All of the servants knew, except Marguerite....I'm not sure where she is now, or I would have brought her here to meet with you."

Mildred paused for a moment and sniffled, looking at Colin and Katherine with frightened eyes.

"It's okay," said Katherine, putting her arm around the upset woman. "We know some of what you're telling us already. But, please, keep going."

Mildred looked at Katherine gratefully and resumed speaking. "It all started about a year ago, after Gregory came back from London. He was so different...he kept talking about this group he belonged to...a vegetarian group. The way he talked about it, it seemed like such a good thing. I'm not sure how it happened, but eventually he converted all of us."

Mildred paused for a moment to wipe away another tear. "Gregory eventually told us about being the heir to the Kingsley fortune. We were all shocked. None of us had any idea. He had plans to turn the estate into an animal sanctuary. It was going to be wonderful. But then, Seth came and poor, dear Gregory went crazy. He felt that all of his plans were going to be ruined! We wanted him to talk to Seth and explain, but he wouldn't. He said we were just going to scare Seth and Cordelia, not hurt them...but now..." Mildred stopping speaking, overcome by her emotions.

"It's okay...everything is going to be okay," said Katherine, leading her away.

Colin looked at Humphries. "Is everything she says true?"

Humphries looked grave. "That's about the whole thing....except for Farnham's London friend, Goldhammer. We never heard of him or met him before, until he showed up yesterday."

Colin nodded his head. Things were becoming clearer to him.

"Humphries," began Colin slowly, "we're going to rescue Cordelia and Seth, and clear up this mystery. But I need your help...listen carefully...this is what I want you and the other servants to do..."

*****

A short time later, Mildred was leading Aunt Dorcas and a large number of guests out of Kingsley Hall. Humphries, Jack, and Connors had joined the throng, bearing wedding gifts out to a waiting car.

"This is ridiculous!" snapped Aunt Dorcas, angrily. "I knew that there was going to be a major disaster. I should have gotten here sooner. I would have made sure everything was up to snuff. But does anyone ever listen to me? Of course not!"

"There, there," replied Mildred, trying to regain her composure under the weight of Dorcas' tirade. "I don't think any of us could have predicted a major plumbing catastrophe. You know how these old houses are....you never know what's going to break. And having everyone stay at the inn in Kingsley Green tonight is only a precaution. Humphries has assured me that the plumbers will be able to fix everything in time for the wedding on Saturday."

"That's right," added Humphries, who was passing by with an armload of gifts. He winked at Mildred, indicating his approval of her explanation. So far Colin's plan was working well. A fictional plumbing problem was the perfect pretense to evacuate the house without all of the guests getting into a panic.

"Humph," said Dorcas, unbelievingly. "I'll believe it when I see it! And what are you imbeciles doing with all of the gifts?

There are a lot of expensive things here. You better not lose anything!"

"We're having all of the gifts moved to the church where the wedding is taking place...just another precaution. We don't want anything to get damaged while the plumbers are working," answered Humphries.

"Hah! Damage!" snorted Dorcas. "I'm sure the gifts will be safer at the church than here. This place is a mess! First my jewels get stolen and then the pipes fall apart...what's next?"

*****

Katherine was standing in the upstairs hallway of Kingsley Hall, waiting for Colin to rejoin her. Her task, which was to find old cousin Wilberforce, was proving to be difficult. Katherine had poked her head into all of his usual haunts on the upper floors of the house, and still there was no sign of him. She was just about to give up, when she heard his distinctive muttering coming from somewhere behind her. Katherine turned, expecting to see the familiar figure of Wilberforce, but, instead, Colin appeared from around the corner.

"Sorry it took me so long," he said, still looking a bit frustrated. "It took longer than I thought to get the servants organized and the house evacuated. And then that idiot Blunderby wouldn't listen to a word I had to say! I ended up having Humphries call him with an anonymous tip about Pembroke, Marguerite, and the robberies. The man is a complete moron....I don't know how he's gotten as far as he has! Chief Inspector...he shouldn't even be on the police force..."

Colin paused a moment in his rant and looked around. "Still no luck finding Wilberforce?" he asked.

"I'm getting closer," said Katherine, walking towards a tapestry that was hanging on the wall in front of her. "I hear him, but I haven't seen him yet. He must be around here somewhere."

Katherine lifted the corner of the tapestry and peered behind it. As she did so, she almost collided with the stooped figure of Wilberforce, who looked as if he had just woken up from a nap.

"Fancy meeting you here," he said to Katherine, as he popped a chocolate-covered nougat into his mouth. "I never met a chameleon I didn't like."

"I really don't see how he's going to help us," whispered Katherine to Colin. "He's batty."

"I'm not sure I agree," said Colin, as he looked at the old man curiously. "He knew about Pembroke and Marguerite. And he seemed to have a good idea that the servants were all part of a secret group. He's also supposed to know every secret corner, hidden stairway, and underground passageway in this place, right?"

"Yes," said Katherine doubtfully, as she watched Wilberforce, who was in the midst of performing a dance that may, in his younger days, have been a jig.

"I have a hunch," said Colin. "I may be wrong, but I think I might know where Cordelia and Seth are being held captive. If he knows as much as you say, he may be the only person who can lead us to them."

"Wilberforce," he said loudly, attempting to attract the attention of the old man.

"What is it? Are you the prime minister my good sir?" Wilberforce demanded, staring fixedly at Colin.

"No, not exactly," replied Colin. But I am here to help Seth and Cordelia. And I was hoping you could lend me a hand."

"Ah, Cordelia" said Wilberforce, a smile overspreading his aged features. "Now, if I was a younger man...."

"Yes, yes," said Colin quickly. "I'm sure we all appreciate Cordelia's finer qualities. However, what I need from you right now is some information that will help us find her...and hopefully save Kingsley Hall in the process. Wilberforce, can you tell me how to get to the underground tunnels beneath the hall?"

"Underground tunnels? Are you crazy my dear boy? I don't know what you're talking about. There are no underground tunnels!"

"We know what everyone says Wilberforce," interjected Katherine soothingly. "But we also know that you know more about this place than anyone. So please, if you can, tell us how we can get to them. It's a matter of life and death!"

"Life and death you say! Well, if it's that important maybe should you ask Jack... the fatted calf!"

"What is he talking about?" whispered Colin to Katherine.

She pulled Colin aside as Wilberforce began to execute another jig.

"He hates Jack... he's the boot boy," explained Katherine, in an undertone. "Cordelia does too. It's because he steals food from the kitchen and eats too much. I think he's trying to bargain with us. We sack Jack and he tells us how to get to the tunnels."

"Oh," said Colin, realization dawning. "He's definitely not as crazy as you think."

"Listen," said Colin to Wilberforce, as he approached the figure of the dancing man. "We'll make sure the boot boy gets the boot, so to speak, if you'll show us how to get to the tunnels."

Wilberforce, who had been capering about like a madman, suddenly snapped to attention. "You've got a deal!" he said energetically. "Follow me!"

CHAPTER 11
THE RESCUE

Is all of this really necessary? asked Farnham pitifully, as he bent over the table to help Goldhammer move the bomb. "Blowing up the house wasn't part of my original plan. I don't want anyone to get hurt"

"It's no longer your plan, my dear fellow," said Goldhammer, with a sneer. "You're now working for me, and for the <u>anarchist</u> group Goldhammer...and as part of that group you're pledged to stamp out hierarchy throughout the world. No governments, no classes, no privilege, no authority of any kind! We aim to live in a stateless, classless society where..."

"But what about the International Society for the Liberation of All Sentient and Insentient Beings? And the animals?" interrupted Farnham. "You never mentioned anything about <u>anarchism</u> to me before."

Goldhammer scoffed, "You really don't mean to tell me you believe all of that nonsense we publish about the animals, do you? We just use that as a cover. None of us really believes any of it! I thought you knew that!"

"I don't understand what you mean," said Farnham, his cherub pink complexion turning deathly pale.

Goldhammer began laughing as he stared unbelievingly at Farnham. "You're really serious aren't you? So you, and all of the servants here, bought all of that animal rights garbage? I don't think I've heard anything so funny in a long time!"

Farnham flushed as Goldhammer continued laughing and then turned away for a moment, his face dark with anger.

"Are you going to help me with this bomb, or not?" snapped Goldhammer impatiently. "We don't have much time left!"

Farnham turned around and looked at Goldhammer coldly.

"No, I'm not going to help you with anything! You tricked me and you lied to me!" he shouted angrily.

Suddenly, Farnham struck out at Goldhammer, rushing at him with all of his force and knocking him down. Goldhammer was completely taken by surprise. Although Goldhammer was the stronger man, Farnham was getting the best of the fight. The two men struggled for a few moments, before Farnham landed a heavy punch that knocked Goldhammer out cold.

In a moment, Farnham was at the side of Cordelia and Seth, untying them and doing his best to apologize.

"It's okay," said Cordelia soothingly, "we understand, don't we Seth?"

As usual, Seth looked confused, but he wasn't about to disagree with Cordelia. "Of course we do," he agreed, uncertainly.

"I'm sorry," said Farnham, hanging his golden head in shame. "It's just that meat is murder, and I didn't know of any other way that I could save the animals if I didn't have the Kingsley estate. I was going to turn Kingsley Hall into an animal sanctuary..."

Cordelia looked thoughtfully at Farnham for a moment, before she replied slowly, "You're right," she said, as if grasping something for the first time. "Meat is made from animals.... I never thought of that before!"

She paused for a moment, still deep in thought, and then began speaking quickly and excitedly. "Farnham, vegetarians can eat chocolate and dessert, can't they?"

"Yes," he said. "It's just meat we're against, not dessert."

"And," she continued eagerly, "there are other good things about being a vegetarian, aren't there?"

"Of course," replied Farnham, "there are lots of reasons to become a vegetarian, besides helping animals. Having a healthier diet, eating more fruits and vegetables..."

"Katherine's always saying I should eat healthier," interrupted Cordelia, "maybe it'd be worth a try."

"Well, if it helps you to decide, you've been a vegetarian since you got here," said Farnham. "Mildred stopped cooking meat ages ago. That's why she was so upset about the meat delivery the first day you were here."

Cordelia's eyes widened. "You're right!" she said, thinking over all of the meals she'd had at Kingsley Hall. "Mildred's such a good cook I didn't even notice!"

Cordelia paused for another moment...it was clear she was making an important decision.

"Farnham," she said with a smile, "we don't have to abandon your plans! I don't want to eat meat if it's made out of animals. That's gross! And with Mildred's incredible cooking I know I won't miss the meat. I'm sure Seth agrees with me. Right Seth?"

Seth still looked lost. Events were moving too fast for him to follow. "Whatever you say dear," he agreed vaguely.

"Kingsley Hall can be an animal sanctuary, we'll become vegetarians, and everyone will be happy."

Farnham beamed at her, not quite believing what he was hearing.

"And," said Cordelia happily, "without all of that meat to fill us up, we'll be able to eat more chocolates and desserts! And fruits and vegetables of course," she added, with a smile.

*****

Cordelia, Seth and Farnham had been chatting for a few moments, when Katherine and Colin rushed into the room.

"Katherine! Colin!" shouted Cordelia happily. "How did

you find us?"

"Wilberforce told us how to get here...we thought we were coming to save you," said Katherine, clearly relieved to see Seth and Cordelia unharmed. "But it looks like you've don't need our help," she added, as she gestured towards the unconscious Goldhammer.

Colin was looking at Farnham suspiciously. "What about this one?" he said. "Isn't he the one who's caused all of this trouble? Should I subdue him?"

"Oh no!" said Cordelia. "Farnham's alright. Or should I say Kingsley.... we're all family now. Anyway, it was just a little misunderstanding. We've figured everything out."

Colin looked unbelievingly from Seth to Cordelia. "Are you sure?" he said, looking at Seth.

"Cordelia seems to have worked things out," said Seth, with a glance at his fiancée. "Although I'm still not sure I understand what's going on."

"Well," said Cordelia, with a smile, "all's well that ends well, as they say. Let's find our way out of here and get on with our wedding."

As Cordelia finished speaking, a small beeping sound was heard coming from the center of the room.

"What is that noise?" said Katherine, looking around.

"Oh no," said Farnham, in despair, "the bomb...the timer must have been activated!"

Everyone in the group looked over at the small contraption. The homemade bomb was flashing and it was clear that some type of countdown was taking place.

"Colin," said Seth slowly, "I don't suppose you know how to defuse a bomb?"

Colin looked pale. "Unfortunately, it's not something they normally teach us in my line of work. It's more of a specialized skill. I doubt that I would be of much help."

Cordelia grabbed Katherine's arm excitedly. "But you can help us Katherine! Didn't you write an "Ask Amaryllis" column a few years ago about defusing bombs? It was something about skills that every modern woman should have, wasn't it?"

Katherine flushed and glared at Cordelia. Despite the circumstances, her authorship of the "Ask Amaryllis" column was a well-guarded secret. Cordelia had been the only one who knew about it, until now. It was not something she wanted anyone to know about, especially not Colin.

"Oops, sorry," said Cordelia, realizing what she had done.

"You write the "Ask Amaryllis" column?" asked Colin softly, looking at Katherine with a strange look on his face.

"Yes," said Katherine, her face red. "But it's a bit embarrassing. Perhaps we could talk about something else?"

"But you don't understand," said Colin. "I'm your biggest fan... I've always wondered who the genius behind Amaryllis was, and now I know."

"I hope you're not making fun of me," said Katherine stiffly.

"I'm completely serious," protested Colin. "Every column is pure genius! The way you slipped those Shakespearean references into your column on removing stains from soiled linens...and all written in iambic pentameter...amazing! And the column on using a map to choose the right road when finding one's way out of a yellow wood...all written in blank verse....it gives me the chills just thinking of it!"

"You noticed that?" said Katherine, in disbelief.

"Of course," said Colin ardently. "I read your column every week and save all of my favorites so I can read them over again."

The two stared at each other for a few moments, as if seeing each other for the first time.

"Um," began Seth apologetically. "I hate to interrupt, but I think the bomb is doing something."

"Oh yes," said Katherine vaguely, the bomb. "Let me take a look."

"Katherine," said Colin doubtfully, as he followed her over to the bomb, "I have great confidence in your abilities, but I don't think I remember an "Ask Amaryllis" column about defusing bombs."

"You wouldn't," said Katherine, as she began fiddling with the wires connected to the front of the homemade contraption, "because that section of the column was cut. You may remember, if you read that particular column, that it was about the most important things every modern woman should be able to do: sewing on a button, ironing a table cloth, and writing a proper thank you note to one's mother-in-law. The last thing, defusing a homemade bomb, was cut by the editor. He didn't think it was appropriate for a woman's magazine. Luckily, I remember how to do it, even though it wasn't published."

Colin gazed at her in awe. This woman was amazing!

"It's a homemade bomb...so it's really not that complicated," Katherine continued. "If you look, there are three wires here...it's just a matter of cutting, clipping, and pulling...all in the right order of course..."

Katherine continued working on the bomb for the next few minutes. That should just about do it," she said, with a smile. "I just have to pull this wire, and we'll be out of the woods."

"Not so fast!" said an unpleasant voice.

"Goldhammer!" said Cordelia, in shock. "You're alive!"

"Of course I'm alive," said Goldhammer scornfully. "You don't think that silly weakling did me any real damage."

"Now my dear," he said, looking at Katherine, "step away from the bomb. We don't want you ruining my plans." As he spoke, he took a small pistol from his pocket and pointed it directly at her.

"You'd better do what he says," said Colin slowly, grabbing Katherine's arm and pulling her away from the bomb.

"That's more like it," said Goldhammer, walking towards the bomb. "Now, we only have a few more minutes before this thing goes off. So if everyone could just sit quietly we'll be done here in no time."

"There's still no way you're going to get away with this," said Seth angrily.

"I think I've heard that line before," said Goldhammer with

a sneer. "And, right now, it does seem that I'm going to get away with it!"

"Oh no you're not!" shouted Farnham, rushing straight towards Goldhammer.

Suddenly, the few dim lights in the room went out, and they were plunged into complete darkness. Cordelia screamed, a gunshot rang out, and then all was silent.

CHAPTER 12
WEDDINGS

Katherine and Colin were standing side by side on a terrace overlooking the grounds of Kingsley Hall. Seth and Cordelia had been married on time, exactly one day after the mysteries at the hall had been cleared up. The two were watching the newly married couple, who were happily laughing and talking near a small pond. Guests were milling about cheerfully, and, from all appearances, the wedding and the party were a great success.

Katherine smiled at Colin as she looked towards Cordelia and Seth. "They look so happy," she said. "You'd never know all that they've been through in the past week."

"It didn't really seem to bother them all that much," said Colin in reply. "But that's the way Seth has always been."

"Cordelia too," said Katherine, in agreement. "I suppose they're perfect for each other in that sense."

"They certainly do have a lot in common," said Colin, as he turned his attention more closely to the couple.

Seth was throwing rocks into the pond, and Cordelia was laughing uproariously each time a rock splashed into the water.

"Don't ask," said Katherine, with a small smile. "They're best appreciated from afar. It's always been too much of a challenge for me to try to understand what they're laughing about."

"You're probably right," agreed Colin. "I don't think I

want to know."

"At least they're here to laugh," said Katherine, with a shudder. "For a little while there, I wasn't sure that we would ever see either of them again. Or you, for that matter! If that bullet had been a little better aimed by Goldhammer you wouldn't be here now."

"It wasn't just Goldhammer's bad aim that saved me," answered Colin. "The bullet wouldn't have been deflected if I hadn't had all of my favorite "Ask Amaryllis" columns in my breast pocket. You saved me!"

"I think it was actually the steel case holding the "Ask Amaryllis" columns that deflected the bullet and saved you," replied Katherine, sensibly.

"You can think what you want," said Colin, with a smile, "but I'm giving credit to you and "Ask Amaryllis" for my survival!"

"Regardless, that was a close call, for all of us," said Katherine.

"I know," agreed Colin. "I just wish I hadn't been so blind! I got thrown off track from the very beginning by the fact that there were two crimes, not just one."

"Well, you figured things out eventually, that's the important part," answered Katherine.

"*We* figured things out, you mean," said Colin, with an appreciative look at Katherine.

"We make quite a team, the two of us."

Katherine looked surprised. "I don't know that I did much to solve the mystery! But I did enjoy working with you," she added, with a small smile. To her own surprise, her first opinion of Colin had changed quite a bit over the past few days.

"I did too," said Colin, with an answering smile.

"And now that we've cleared up all of the mysteries," asked Katherine, "what's going to happen to everyone? Farnham, the servants, Goldhammer, and Percy... I assume they'll all be punished in one way or another. I feel the worst for poor

Farnham... he's such a dear."

"Farnham is going to be treated at an institution," Colin answered. "I think he might be certifiably crazy. Although it's clear that he and the other servants didn't know anything about Goldhammer's <u>anarchist</u> group. They really believed they were part of a vegetarian association. But, I don't think you have to feel too badly for Farnham. From what I can gather, Cordelia seems set on having him back here as soon as possible. She considers him to be Seth's long lost brother and just as much a Kingsley as Seth himself. Plus, since Seth and Cordelia have decided to become vegetarians, Farnham's plans for Kingsley Hall are still going to happen, even without his inheriting the estate, which apparently he never cared about anyway. He just wanted to make the place into an animal sanctuary."

"And Goldhammer?" asked Katherine. "I feel like he's the real criminal in this whole mess."

"Ah, Goldhammer," said Colin, with a satisfied smile. "I still can't believe that he's finally going to come to justice. He'll probably be put on trial in a few months. And, with all of the evidence we have against him, I wouldn't be surprised if he's put away for a very long time."

"That's a relief!" answered Katherine. I wouldn't want to run into him again anytime soon! I'm glad he's the only one that's going to be brought to trial. I don't think the other servants really meant to do anything wrong...they were just misguided by Farnham."

"I'm fairly certain they'll think twice again before getting involved in any crazy schemes," replied Colin. "From what I understand, Humphries is putting an end to his playboy lifestyle and finally settling down with Mildred. He proposed last evening. And, Connors has sworn off joining any associations, especially vegetarian ones, for the near future. He has his hands full with Jack anyway. As per our agreement with Wilberforce, Jack has been exiled from the kitchen and is now being employed as Connors' assistant in the stables. Jack's already eaten his way through a large part of the feed used for the horses...who knows what he'll be eating next!"

"I'm not surprised," replied Katherine with a smile. "That boy will eat anything!"

"So I suppose that just leaves our jewel thieves," added Katherine.

"They'll both be facing fairly lengthy sentences as well," replied Colin. "Thanks to our anonymous tip, Percy and Marguerite were caught in the very act of stealing all of Seth and Cordelia's wedding presents from the church. Plus, I think with the evidence that the police found at Pembroke's cottage, including the Van Sant jewels and Cordelia's engagement ring, they can be connected to a whole string of robberies across the country. We've made the land a much safer place by catching them."

"It's still incredible to me that we even caught them at all!" said Katherine. "Percy was very circumspect. And Marguerite! Everyone thought she was just a really hard worker! Who would have ever suspected that she was using the laundry as a way to carry stolen goods out of the house? The two of them could have escaped with all of the jewels and who knows what else before anyone figured out that they were the thieves!"

"Ah," replied Colin happily, "but greed was their downfall! I knew that if we set them up they would take the bait. Once they heard that the gifts were being moved to the church in Kingsley Green, they couldn't resist. And that allowed Blunderby to catch them red handed!"

"It was nice that you let Blunderby and Davis, Jr. take credit for all of the arrests," said Katherine. "You didn't have to do that."

"No," said Colin, with a smile. "But poor Blunderby was so convinced that we were behind all of the disturbances at Kingsley Hall. I don't think he could have dealt with the double disappointment of not being able to arrest us and not getting any credit for arresting the real thieves. It's fine with me if everyone thinks he was the mastermind who unraveled the whole mystery."

Katherine laughed. "I doubt anyone who really knows Blunderby believes he solved the mystery! But it's nice you're letting him bask in the glory for a little while."

"It was the least I could do," replied Colin, with a smile.

Katherine paused for a moment and then sighed. "It's strange to think that all of this is over. I suppose I'll have to figure out what to do with myself now."

"Do you have any plans?" asked Colin, softly.

"Well," replied Katherine, "Cordelia and Seth have asked me to stay here with them, but that doesn't feel quite right. I should go back to America, but I don't really know what's there for me. "Ask Amaryllis" and living with Aunt Dorcas don't seem very appealing."

"You wouldn't think about working with me?" asked Colin, hesitantly.

"What do you mean... working with you?" said Katherine, not sure she understood what he meant.

"It's not every investigator that gets the chance to have the woman behind "Ask Amaryllis" on his side," said Colin gently, with a sparkle in his eye. "You don't think I would pass up such an opportunity."

"What exactly are you asking me, Colin?" said Katherine, her face suddenly turning pale.

"I'm asking you to be my wife," he replied, seriously.

Katherine was shocked into speechlessness. She knew that Colin had warmed to her since their first encounter, but marriage! The idea had never occurred to her!

"Did you ask her yet?" said Cordelia, as she and Seth walked up to the terrace excitedly. "You better say yes," she added, with a stern glance at Katherine, "or I'll never forgive you."

Katherine was still overcome by shock. "I don't know what to say..." she began haltingly.

"How about yes!" said Cordelia impatiently.

Katherine took a deep breath, and then smiled shyly. "For once I think I'll have to agree with you," said Katherine to

Cordelia.

She looked straight into Colin's eyes, gave him her hand, and whispered, "Yes."

THE END?

KATHERINE'S LIST OF WORDS YOU MAY NOT KNOW

(THE GLOSSARY)

Advocating

to write or speak in favor of, to publicly support.

Alliance

to form a union of individuals that combine efforts towards a common goal.

Aloof

at a distance, especially in feelings or interests, to stand apart.

Anarchist

a person who wants to overthrow by violence all forms of government, without a purpose of establishing any other system of order to replace the one destroyed.

Avid

showing enthusiasm or great interest in.

Befitted

to be proper for, appropriate, to suit, to fit.

Befuddled

to confuse, as with idle comments or irrelevant arguments.

Breach

to break or rupture.

Brooding

to obsess over morbid, depressing, or painful thoughts or memories.

Cherub

a beautiful or innocent person, especially a child.

Circumspect

watchful and discreet; cautious; prudent.

Coherently

logically connected; consistent. Harmonious in structure.

Condescended

to behave as if one is conscious of descending from a superior position, or higher rank.

Conscientious

careful, cautiously guided by one's sense of what is correct, just, and right.

Consequence

the affect, result, or outcome of some earlier event.

Contemptuous

showing disdain, or scornful disrespect.

Deemed

to form an opinion, to judge, regard.

Dejectedly

to be depressed in spirit; disheartened.

Demeanor

behavior, conduct.

Deplorable

causing or being the subject of regret; lamentable.

Derisively
in a manner expressing contempt or ridicule.

Devastated
to lay waste; to render desolate.

Disdainfully
showing of scorn.

Disgruntled
displeased and discontented.

Disheveled
hanging loosely in disorder; unkempt.

Dismissively
indicating rejection; to remove from consideration often flippantly.

Distracted
to divert attention.

Eerie
spooky; uncanny, so as to inspire superstitious fear.

Elaborate
ornate; marked with intricate and often excessive detail; complicated.

Endeavor
to exert oneself; to make an effort; strive.

Energetically
showing an abundance of energy.

Ensconced
to settle in snuggly, to be securely covered.

Evasive
seeking to evade, prevent from discovering truth.

Exaggerating
To magnify beyond truth, overstate.

Exasperation
state of annoyance, or irritation.

Exuberance
state of enthusiasm, very joyful.

Exuded
to display abundantly and conspicuously.

Fascinated
in a state of aroused curiosity, intrigued.

Fruitless
unproductive, useless.

Guffaw
unrestrained burst of laughter.

Harassing
to pester, to persistently disturb, to torment.

Harmonious
pleasant, agreeing in feeling, action, or attitude.

Hesitantly
undecided, doubtful, or disinclined.

Hideous
very ugly, repulsive.

Hierarchy
any system of people or things ranked one above the other.

Horrific
something that causes shock or horror.

Immaculately
completely clean, without spots or stains.

Incomprehensible
impossible to be understood or comprehended.

Incredulously
in a manner indicating disbelief.

Inept
without skill or aptitude.

Ingratiates
to take action that puts you in the good graces of others.

Inquiries
a seeking of truth, knowledge, or information.

Insufferable
unbearable, not to be endured, intolerable.

Intrigued
a state of aroused curiosity, fascinated.

Lavish
to give in great amounts.

Lingered
to stay longer than expected.

Melancholy
depression, a gloomy disposition, usually over a long period.

Obsessed
to be completely preoccupied with a single topic.

Overbearing
rudely arrogant, dictatorial.

Overwhelmed
to be overcome completely in thought or feeling.

Pompous
haughty, to make a display of one's own importance.

Portly
rather heavy, fat, chubby.

Pursuit
an effort to attain, to chase after.

Rendezvous
a meeting at an agreed time and place, typically between two people.

Reserved
set apart for special occasions, or a particular purpose.

Resolutely

with firm resolve, determination.

Resonant

resounding, echoing, amplified.

Reverts

to return to a former state or owner.

Rub

something that annoys, or irritates another.

Scullery

a small room, normally near the kitchen where food is portioned, or utensils are stored.

Serene

peaceful, quiet.

Skulked

to move stealthily.

Smitten

very much in love.

Solitude

state of being alone.

Specifies

stated clearly and in detail, so there is no confusion.

Subdue

to overpower with superior force.

Suppress

to repress, put an end to the activities of someone.

Tactfully
to avoid causing offense.

Tainted
to be blemished slightly, a trace of contamination.

Technicalities
small details, often trivial.

Tirade
a long outburst of negative speech.

Transformed
to change in form, or structure, to morph.

Trivial
insignificant detail, of very little importance.

Ulterior
to have motives other than those expressed, to conceal the true desire.

Unorthodox
not conforming to rules, not proceeding in the expected manner.

Vindictively
inclined to revenge, spite, to be vengeful.

Look for other books by author Kerry Marie Sloan

Witches Academy

The Guardian Series by author Kerry Marie Sloan

The Book of Westmere
The Four Towers